Guthrie's Lot Part 1:

A Spacious Place

Olwyn Harris

Reading Stones Publishing

Published by: Reading Stones Publishing
                Helen Brown & Wendy Wood
Cover Design: Wendy Wood

For more copies contact the publisher at:

Glenburnie Homestead
212 Glenburnie Road
ROB ROY NSW 2360
Mobile: 0422 577 663
Email: hbrown19561@gmail.com

For Helen, my teacher, who opened up the pages of possibilities and gave space to my writing. Thank you for being part of this journey!

A Spacious Place

He reached down from on high
and took hold of me;
He drew me out of deep waters.
The LORD was my support.
He brought me out into a spacious place;
He rescued me because he delighted in me.

(Psalm 18:16,19)

Olwyn Harris

1893

1.

"Hello? Mr Guthrie? My name is Joanna Grenham. I have a letter of introduction. Reverend Brasheur's wife told me you have been looking for a carer without much success. I am here to offer my services until you can find someone suitable." She watched the cart disappear down the track in the evening shadows and thought she was being shipwrecked on a deserted island, watching her lifeboat vanish past the horizon.

Irvin looked at her slender fitting dress and her fancy bonnet and frowned. "Hmm," he said noncommittally.

Joanna waited for a time, but he stood there and said nothing further. His large frame reinforced every impression Mrs Brasheur had given her. She was here to offer respite and relief in the manner of a missionary being sent to the ignorant savages of the dark continents. She shuddered and pulled her fringed shawl in a little tighter as the sun dipped low and lost all its warmth. The wind blew leaves across the clearing with a desolate moan. "Did Reverend Brasheur tell you I would be coming?"

He nodded. "He did."

"Oh. Well, that is a relief. I was thinking that perhaps you were not expecting me. Ahh... I understand you have a daughter, and you would like some help while your wife recovers. Oh, and the Reverend said that your order from the general store had already been put together and thought he would save you a trip into town by sending it out with me."

"Did he now?" He stared at the box with a frown.

She could see he was uncomfortable with this deed of goodwill. "I considered that a sympathetic gesture, given how busy you are with the farm and your family," Joanna said.

"Did you now?" He raised a brow at her, picked up the box in one arm and her suitcase in the other. "Well. Come in," he said as he pushed opened the door. The doorway was low and he stooped to go inside. The murky glass lamp was not lit, and the hut was gloomy; the air was stale and the shadows cold. Mrs Guthrie was sitting in a sturdy upholstered chair that was of a finer quality than the other furniture in the hut. Some knitting lay idle in her lap. A girl was wrapped in a thin rug hugging a cat, lying in front of a bunk that was jammed up against the wall. She was drawing, straining her eyes against the shadows.

"Bonnie. Stoke the fire. We'll eat." He grunted as he hung up his hat and coat, and then lit a lamp on the table. It smoked badly. The wick was in need of a trim.

Joanna looked around, dismay filling every fibre of her slight figure. There were dishes piled unwashed on the table. Clutter lined the dresser and everything just sort of looked... used. She cringed as the girl jumped up to stir the stew. She wiped a dry dirty bowl with a dry dirty rag and ladled stew from the pot and passed it to her father. He swiped some things to the side so he could sit at the table and proceeded to eat his meal.

Bonnie did the ritual again and passed the bowl to her. Joanna quickly held up her hand. "Oh no thank you. I've already eaten. I packed a sandwich for the trip." She removed her bonnet and held it in her lap as she sat at the table, stiff and uncomfortable.

Bonnie shrugged and diverted her offering to her mother, who sat silently in the corner. And then she served herself. Irvin looked up at Joanna. "We ain't fancy people here," he said as he slurped stew from his spoon, eyeing the bonnet that she hung onto as if it was some sort of lifebuoy.

"I can see that," she said grimly.

"Humph." He slurped more stew a little louder, looking at her across the rim of his bowl, daring her to stay. He nodded to the chair in the corner. "My wife: Adele." She nodded and coughed a breathless acknowledgment. "And that's Bonnie." He stood up and took a second helping of stew, and then slopped the leftovers into a dish on the floor.

A dog ambled over and helped himself. "Dog's name is Tuck." Introductions were complete.

"Well Sir, if you could show me where I will be sleeping, I will unpack. I will start my duties in the morning if that is agreeable. I am tired from the trip."

He grunted again, with a roll of his eyes. "We're all tired." Then he angled his jaw towards a limp curtain. "Bonnie's cot is behind there. You take that. Bonnie, you sleep out here." He nodded towards a day bed in the corner beside Mrs Guthrie's chair. Bonnie obliged by kicking off her shoes, dragging the thin rug off the floor with her, and climbing under the patched covers. He scraped his chair out and lumbered over to his wife. Joanna closed her eyes and shuddered. She opened her eyes as he murmured gently, and then paused as she watched him help her up. He was tender and patient as she leant on his arm. He guided her towards a curtained divider, and he drew it aside. She could see in the shadows that their bed was made from plain rough sawn timber, the covers worn. He turned around and saw her watching them. He nodded with a frown. "'Night then." And he dropped the curtain down shrouding their privacy.

Joanna took the lantern and pulled back the curtain to the booth that was designated as her quarters. The bed was low and the mattress thin. There was one small dresser and she opened the drawers. They were crammed full of rags, linen and an assortment of family clothes in no particular order. She opened her suitcase on the floor and pulled out fresh sheets. She re-made the bed and put the used linen to the side. She went to the stove and poured some water into a bowl. She couldn't find a towel, so used a clean petticoat to complete her ablutions. It all seemed very inadequate. How was she supposed to make a difference in a hovel like this?

Reverend Brasheur had assured her with sincere Christian conviction that the situation was needful. The temporary placement would be short lived because he was following up with a very likely prospect of an experienced carer. Two weeks, three at the most. That encouraged her. She would clean and sort and ready this place for the arrival of the nurse. That way, at least Mrs Guthrie would be able to rest, and be comforted with the knowledge that her household was running smoothly awaiting the arrival of the proper placement. Surely that would alleviate her mind.

Joanna shivered in the dark, and a draught blew in between the slabs in the wall. She put on a jumper, then laid her travel coat over her bed... and then as an after-thought pulled on another pair of socks. She looked around the curtain at Bonnie curled up in a ball under the thin covers. She went over to the hook by the door and took the overcoat hanging there and tucked it over Bonnie's shoulders. Then she lay down and tried to think warm thoughts in a cold and desolate place. Why did she ever agree to do this favour for Reverend Brasheur and his wife? They seemed so genuinely concerned for their cousin. All she could see was this was going to be a very long uncomfortable couple of weeks.

❧~❦☙❧~❦

2.

Joanna woke to the sound of wood chopping and Mrs Guthrie coughing. It took her a moment to think where she actually was. It came in a rush. She closed her eyes again and took a deep breath. The air was stale and cold. But then: didn't Scripture say God's mercies are new every morning? And this was a new day. She believed it was a true observation that life generally seems clearer in the fresh air of morning. She got out of bed, wrapped herself up warmly and pulled on her gloves. She went out and stoked the fire and put the kettle on to boil. She opened the door and stared as the morning sun peeked over the hills. The dull yards and drab buildings were transformed in a sparkling white overlay, as a million diamantes of frost icicles sprinkled the bush surrounds glittering in the morning light. Its pristine beauty took her breath away. How incredibly majestic! Her artistic eye absorbed every shadow and highlight as the dawn of sunrise, fresh and crisp, flowed across the valley.

Her attention was pulled back to the grimy shack behind her as Mrs Guthrie's coughing, raspy and harsh, shattered the moment. Smoke was quickly filling the hut. Damp wood and probably a blocked flue in the little stove was choking the shack with smoke. She quickly propped open the shutter and frantically waved her apron to try and clear the haze.

Joanna looked around and wondered what possibilities might be available for breakfast. She found a bag of oatmeal on the shelf and a basket of eggs on the sill. She put some lard in the frying pan and set about cooking the eggs. The fourth egg she cracked ruptured in a rank smear all over the pan. She quickly took the pan outside, gagging at the smell. When she tipped it out, Tuck came and helped himself to the putrid spoils. The irony struck her. She was anticipating fresh morning air and new blessings; what she got was a smoky hut and rotten eggs. She leant over, retching into the kerchief she held over her mouth.

Mr Guthrie was staring at her from the wood heap with a frown. "We never crack eggs straight into the pan. You don't know what you are going to get." He muttered his disapproval to the kindling. Spoiling the good eggs was an unnecessary waste when they already had a skimpy pantry! He bemoaned his plight and the inconvenience of having struck his own rotten egg roulette with this invasion of his household. He muttered his additional observation that apparently basic common-sense couldn't possibly come dressed in a swanky skirt. It was hardly welcome! He gathered the tinder he was splitting and commented to the sparrows as he walked past that he didn't think that being sensible, plain-and-simple, to be an unrealistic expectation.

"I'll remember to break the eggs in a cup next time," Joanna said curtly and followed him inside.

Mr Guthrie dumped tomorrow's kindling on the hearth. The fire was smothered; smoke pouring out of every crack around the stove. "Damn possum is in the chimney again. Bonnie – bring me the poke. Pass it up when I am on the roof."

Joanna's eyes were smarting from the smoke and she watched wide-eyed as Mr Guthrie open up a flue-flap near the top of the stove, more smoke spewed forth. She followed him outside and watched as he quickly scaled the wall of his hut using a trestle that created an improvised ladder to the roof. Huh. His agility was unexpected given his large frame.

Bonnie dragged over a long, thin pole, and Joanna helped her tip it on its end so he could reach it. He threaded it down the chimney and vigorously gave its occupant an inhospitable prod. Bonnie dragged Joanna back inside, and called out to her father. There was an objectionable screech from inside the flue. Joanna jumped back as a black sooted possum tumbled out the vent; landed on its feet like the proverbial cat with nine lives; gave and unearthly hiss; and skedaddled across the table and benches and dived out the propped open shuttered window leaving a trail of ash and scattered stuff behind it. Its brushed tail was raised like a flag of surrender in its retreat, as it disappeared over the sill.

Joanna held onto the back of a chair in total shock and took some slow deep shuddering breaths. She landed in some sort of nightmare! Was this place completely possessed?

Mr Guthrie raised his brow as he came inside and wordlessly went about setting the kindling, obviously less than bothered that the disturbance had rattled this visitor. He lit the fire, brushed the soot and ashes into a pan without a pause. And then he spoke over his shoulder as went to tend to his wife; her coughing continued unabated from the bedroom. "You'll be fixing some breakfast then." It was not a question.

"Oh yes. Right," said Joanna taking a shuddering breath. This must be what a normal Guthrie morning looks like. "Back to breakfast." There were not enough eggs now, so Joanna retrieved the bag of flour delivered in the box of supplies yesterday and made up some plain pancakes with the remaining eggs: each one cracked carefully into a cup first. This morning was not exactly what she had been hoping. She had wanted to break the ice with some good nourishment to impress her way into this desperate family. She had not cracked the frosty reception; that was certain.

All she had managed was a rotten egg and breaking some non-negotiable rules she never even knew had existed.

She found four plates and washed them in heated water. Then she cleared the table, wiping the sooty paw prints away before she set it for breakfast. Mrs Guthrie came out of the bedroom when the pancakes were served, coughing through the smoky haze that still refused to clear, and breathlessly took her seat. "Good morning, Mrs Guthrie. It is a brisk morning today. I trust the hut will soon warm with the fire going." Joanna always believed in presenting an optimistic air even though it didn't seem likely that her confidence would be rewarded the way the door and windows were propped wide open.

Mr Guthrie returned with another armful of firewood. He closed the door and sat wordlessly the table. He stared grimly at the pancakes, burnt around the edges, piled on the plate. When he started to fork a pancake or two onto his plate, Joanna cleared her throat. "I would like to say Grace before we eat. It is a good example for the children and a policy of gratitude for ourselves." She bowed her head and closed her eyes. Mrs Guthrie paused, nodded to Bonnie and they both followed her example.

Mr Guthrie froze mid-air. Put down his fork and pursed lips. Joanna closed her eyes and waited. The man of the house always offered the blessing. She glanced up at him with a raised brow. He nodded impatiently with a frown for her to proceed. "Well, get on with it then."

"Oh. Okay. Thank you, Heavenly Father, for your bounteous provision. Bless this food and this household with your good health. Amen."

Mr Guthrie grunted. "*Bounteous*? That's rich,"

"Amen," wheezed Mrs Guthrie. The rest of the meal was taken in silence. Joanna tentatively asked a couple of questions about the expectations of the day, but was received with an unmannerly snort from Mr Guthrie, and silence from Mrs Guthrie and Bonnie. She quickly chose silence as well.

It wasn't long before Mr Guthrie gulped the last of his drink and stood to his feet. "I'll be back on sundown. Bonnie will help ye with whatever you need." And he went to the door, stood for a moment and turned impatiently. "Where is my coat?"

Joanna quickly retrieved it from Bonnie's bunk. "It was cold last night," she said as she handed it to him.

"Was it now? It was cold this morning as well, so put it back if you take it. I need it for my morning chores," he said. Then he left to do whatever farmer-ing thing he needed to do.

Joanna felt the bank of thunderclouds of his disapproval gathering across the horizon as she watched him stride over to their large shed. He might be tall. He might be strong. But what a miserable man! Little wonder the Reverend and his wife were so mindful of her cousin's needs. She turned to Mrs Guthrie. "Where would you like me to start this morning Ma'am?"

"Adele. Call me Adele," she wheezed.

"Oh. Very well. Adele."

"Bonnie. Take the bucket and fetch the water please." Her daughter nodded reluctantly and pulled on her boots. She went outside with her bucket tramping boot prints through the frost that would not start dissolving in the cold morning sun until much later.

Joanna turned to her apologetically. "Mrs Guthrie... Adele... I'm sorry, but I don't think your husband likes me being here. I just want to reassure you that I am only here to help you as an interim measure. Reverend Brasheur assures me that they are organising a permanent nurse to come. She will be much more suitable to your needs."

"I am grateful. Irvin is grateful." She paused to catch her breath.

Joanna remembered the grim line of his brow and didn't think gratitude was any part of Mr Guthrie's mindset. "Well, I am only here for a short time until a proper carer can be found, so I will do what I can until she arrives. Besides, when the warmer weather comes, I'm sure your health will improve."

"I want Bonnie to have classes. Reading and writing. Can you do that?"

"School? Oh really? Could I?" She smiled with surprise. "I didn't think I was here for that... but certainly, whatever you need!" She said that with more enthusiasm than she intended. She paused and reigned in her buoyancy as she looked around the hut. "How about... we do some housework, and then make a plan for the next two weeks that includes lessons for Bonnie. If we establish a routine it will be easier for the nurse to settle in when she gets here."

Adele smiled. "Yes. I'd like that. I want Bonnie to learn."

"I can definitely help with that. I saw you knitting yesterday. What is your project?"

"Nothing really... just squares... it keeps my hands busy and I find it hard to do anything more just now..."

"How many have you completed? Would there be enough to start piecing a rug for Bonnie? It was so cold last night."

Adele pointed to a low box beside her chair. There was a pile of squares spilling over the brim. "I'm nearly out of yarn... and I've not got to spinning more." She nodded towards a wheel sitting in the corner, covered in web and hidden under clutter.

"Do you have extra fleece?"

"In the shed. We kept a bale or two."

Light lit up Joanna's eyes. "How about..." So she started developing a standard routine: housework in the morning; lessons after lunch before starting the afternoon chores. There were a myriad of things to address: washing clothes; washing linen; sweeping; dusting; washing up; stacking dresser shelves; sorting drawers; beating out mats; and making dinner. Adele started hand sewing some of her squares together with the remaining yarn, while Joanna and Bonnie sang their way around the hut in their cleaning frenzy. It seemed a lot was achieved, but even Joanna conceded, a small hut with only two curtained areas was not too demanding.

After lunch, Adele lay down and rested. Joanna sat quietly with Bonnie at the table and went over what she knew of her alphabet letters. If this was the petition of a mother, then it was request she would honour. They started with a small piece of charcoal from the ash-heap and a plain sheet of paper that Joanna pulled from her stationery set. Basic, but practical. "Now I want you write out your letters as carefully as you can."

"Okay Miss Grenham," said Bonnie shyly.

"That is perfect. Now let's try some words. Say the letters as you write them."

Eventually Adele stirred from her nap, and they cleared their work off the table to set it ready for dinner.

When Mr Guthrie came in and hung his hat and coat on the hook by the door, he stood for a moment, staring at the transformed living area. Adele sat in her chair. The empty grocery box was standing on its end beside her, covered with a small cloth and a couple of items sitting there for easy access including a cup of water. She was sewing together her squares and was determined to finish the row. She looked up and beamed at her husband as he stood there. "We have been busy," she said.

"That you have," he said quietly. He came over and hunkered down in front of her chair. "Not doing too much?"

"Joanna is quite determined that I rest. We are getting a routine established before her replacement comes. She says it will help my recovery. Bonnie? Show your father what you have done today." She stopped and paused, already breathless, and started coughing.

Bonnie came over with her sheet of letters. She held it up for her father to see. She very proudly spoke out some of the letters and words she was learning.

"Quite the student." He turned to Joanna. "Have you nothing to show me too?"

She raised her brow and thought that it had been obvious what she had been doing. Instead, she nodded and said, "Only dinner, Mr Guthrie. If it is edible, that will be achievement enough. I am no cook." He gave a wry chuckle and didn't disagree.

Each night Mr Guthrie helped his wife over to the table and when they were all seated, they waited as Joanna said grace. Then Joanna ladled the stew into bowls and Bonnie passed them around. Joanna quickly learned to come to the table armed with questions: what was a highlighted moment in their day; a challenge; and a smile? Her cajoling to answer these prompts seemed far more successful than the stoic silence or monosyllabic responses her first experiences elicited. She continued to piece together more about the farm and this family over their evening meals.

This night Mr Guthrie helped himself to another serving and returned to the table. "So what about you?"

Joanna looked up from her bowl. "What about me?"

"Every meal you ask each one of us about our day: but what about you? What was your highlight; challenge; and smile?"

"Oh." This was unexpected, and for some reason it was uncomfortable for her to be included. She swallowed and took a breath. "Well. Highlight: to see Bonnie becoming familiar with her letters and numbers. I've wanted to be a teacher since I could hold a book, so this is definitely a highlight. Challenge... cooking. That stove is a cantankerous old woman who just does what she wants."

Irvin chuckled. "Sounds like two of a kind. You should get along."

Joanna quickly glanced over at him, and saw he was looking at Adele with a grin. She took a breath and smiled. "Okay. But I do admire Adele's patience in stepping me through her recipes. And my smile... well, ahh... today... it was using a spinning-wheel again. It is a long time since I have done spinning... and Adele told me that my plain-spun yarn may be more useful as baling twine to tie up your hay-stooks. However, I insist it is very suitable for knitting because we need very thick rugs."

Adele reached across and patted her hand with a tired chuckle. "That was my smile too. I have never seen yarn so. I think you will need to keep your tutoring job."

෴෧ා୦ଷ෴

When Joanna opened her eyes, she quickly glanced outside and smiled delightedly: sunrays were spilling over the horizon. A sunny day. They could try that walk today! Something was always thwarting her plan... rain, an unpleasant wind, Adele having a 'wheezy' day, or chores that needed more urgent attention. They finished breakfast and Mr Guthrie left for the paddocks. She and Bonnie whizzed through their morning routine, each task a springboard to mathematical problem solving or spelling quizzes. Bonnie had a quick mind and soaked up Joanna's tutoring like a sponge. By lunchtime they had a small picnic in hand, and they rugged up and went to find Mr Guthrie to surprise him with a snack. They walked along the track where they could see him ploughing a newly cleared section of paddock with his two mules named Aaron and Hur. Adele said she had named the mules after the two men in the Bible who supported Moses arms to be raised in prayer so that the battle they were fighting could be won. These mules were the greatest support in helping them in their life here. Joanna appreciated that choice of names. She knew the story. "We all need someone to hold us up and support us when are fighting hard to make progress," she agreed.

Joanna prompted Bonnie to notice bushland curiosities with the eye of an artist: the blue on the kookaburras' wing as they sat laughing at each other on a branch; the cluster of kangaroos lazing in the sun with their legs sprawled out behind them; the gum trees standing stately and tall, their evergreen leaves dressing them elegantly, in the stark contrast to the skeletal frames of the deciduous trees around them. There were all sorts of marvels to notice. Joanna admired how beautiful the farm was in this raw, uncensored, untamed state. She had never had the opportunity to see this through the lens of the people who lived in the rough. There was something quite majestic about it. She turned to Adele. "I think I understand more why you chose to come and live out here, away from town. It seems like a hard choice to me, but it is also a very dignified one. The beauty of this place is quite profound."

"Thank you," she said. "My cousin considers my decision to marry Irvin to be far below my station and disposition. She blames him for my health, and I have been relegated to the designation of "poor country cousin", the one who lost her way. But you are right: to be here with the people I love has not been a sacrifice. When I came out here… Irvin built this hut for us. I thought it was a palace. No one had ever made such an effort just for me. He was so determined that we would improve it and make it better. But then… life gets in the way. Still, it is a blessing regardless of how hard some of it has been."

By the time they found a protected spot out of the wind, in the sun, and laid out the blanket, Adele was quite fatigued and lay down on the rug to have a rest. Joanna brought out her art folder and sat beside her making some sketches: a study of the mule-team ploughing the furrows; a tall tree denuded by the cold, its branches creating a fine silhouette of lace against the cold stone-blue of the sky; a wren picking at insects in the tall dry winter grass.
Bonnie spent some time running around exploring with Tuck and had a game by tossing him a stick. It really was the perfect winter's day.

When it was time for lunch, Bonnie ran over to her father and invited him to come and join them. Joanna quickly put away her sketches and served their baked bread with salted beef. The loaf was stodgy, but it was soon demolished anyway, along with the oatmeal biscuits they had baked, fringed with a dark overcooked edge. Joanna stood up, and gathered Bonnie to go in search of some nature samples to study. She glanced back and saw Mr Guthrie reclining beside his wife, fiddling with a blade of grass, smiling in a privately shared moment. She blushed a little and turned away. Adele's disclosure gave her a different way to look at this family. Sacrifice and determination and care. That was more of what she would like in a husband, rather than the starched collars and straight-backed chairs that were the prevailing standard of the sitting room in the manse where she boarded. Reverend Brasheur would never relax enough to even stretch his legs out in front of a fire. No, she decided, she respected Adele's choice. A wide-open space under a clear blue sky with a man you love, that was preferable over the social respectability of a stuffy living room with high-backed upholstered chairs any day.

∾⊱⊰∾

3.

Joanna sat at the manse dining table and bowed her head while Reverend Brasheur said grace. As the Amen closed the prayer, she opened her eyes and took the napkin from the table setting. It was a relief to eat a meal with the normal comforts of home at her disposal. Their visitor, Mr Thomas, was an amiable distraction as well. He could almost hold a conversation without having to prompt every response.

She poured drinks from the crystal decanter on the tray in the centre of the table and noticed more acutely than ever, the extreme social divide between the Brasheurs and Guthries. Joanna had considered that the Reverend was generous to take responsibility for the remuneration of Adele's carer. His wife had patiently explained how their support paid tribute to the regard they held for their relative. But now she wondered if Adele's insight was closer to the truth. Perhaps their interference was more accurately a condescending attempt to rescue their 'poor lost country cousin' to offset the neglect of her 'stubborn, uncivilised' husband. She had heard that accusation often enough.

"How did you find my cousin Joanna-dear? I trust she is much improved?"

"I fear she is still very frail, Mrs Brasheur. She has a very persistent and vexing cough. I believe that Doctor

Fredricks has made some recommendations regarding her ongoing recuperation."

Mrs Brasheur looked up from her soup and scowled as if she had just swallowed a large dose of quinine. "We have not been inattentive to my cousin's needs! After all, we have done everything we could, to compensate for that man's ruthless disregard for her delicate constitution!"

"I did not mean to suggest..."

"Doctor Fredricks knows our concern for the situation."

"I am sure that he does."

"He certainly does. We continue to do what we can!"

"Her lack of improvement in no way implies your neglect."

"It certainly does not. She should not be living out there in the boondocks in the first place! It is so uncivilised."

Joanna thought to try and divert the direction of the conversation. "How are the enquiries for the nurse progressing? I have been out there for over six weeks now, so I trust that time provided you with some suitable applications"

Mrs Brasheur glanced at her husband who nodded thoughtfully with a frown. "Yes. Yes, I believe there has been progress," he murmured.

"Oh that is wonderful news! Has she arrived? I was hoping that I could meet with her and explain some of

Ade… your cousin, Mrs Guthrie's needs." This couple never referred to Adele by her Christian name, regardless of their insistence of their persisting affection. Her humiliating choice to connect herself with this degrading situation was not to be forgotten.

Reverend Basheur put down his soup-spoon and cleared his throat. "You have met Mr Thomas?"

Joanna was in no mood to accommodate this irrelevant detour. "Yes. Of course. We met earlier." Mrs Brasheur had seated them together with pointed remarks about their varied common interests. Joanna suspected Mrs Brasheur was hopeful of a romantic alliance, but Mr Thomas was so young the idea was entirely ridiculous. Once they had spoken of the school he attended, the bleakness of the winter weather and touched on the controversy of reading William Blake there seemed little else of mutual interest to talk about. Although he did enthusiastically share a few tales of the antics of Dasher, the family dog he left behind. Whenever Joanna nodded benignly, he was encouraged to share yet another story. It seemed his storehouse of anecdotes concerning Dasher's adventures was not poorly stocked.

The Reverend cleared his throat again. "Mr Thomas has been appointed as the new School Master."

Joanna choked and put down her spoon. Her head flung back like she had been slapped. No softening that blow. "School Master? You have already engaged him as your teacher? This process has been stalled for months!"

Mrs Brasheur quickly responded. "Well you were away for such an extended time Joanna-dear ... and we really had to move on this situation. Like you said, it has been going on way too long."

"I was away for six weeks! Because you said you had not been able to find a nurse sooner." She turned towards the Reverend who sat at the head of the table focused intently on buttering his bread. "You told me that I would be able to submit my application on my return. You promised me I would have the opportunity to at least apply!"

Mr Thomas swallowed and looked as if he wanted to dive into his soup and drown. Joanna stared at those around the table. "The carer has not come at all, has she?"

"Well, we did ask for a woman, but since Mr Thomas came from the academy instead, we considered this a divine intervention from the Hand of Providence. And since you are already settled out at Guthrie's place, it seemed expedient to..."

"Settled? I went out there as a favour to you both! I made it perfectly clear I am not available to be placed there permanently. I have been telling them that a suitable appointment would be coming soon. Now they have no one."

"You should go back. That would be appropriate."

"No I cannot! This is outrageous! You have not been forthcoming with me at all."

"Joanna – let us eat our meal in cordial fellowship. We can discuss this matter later, in a congenial manner, fitting of respectable adults." The Reverend picked up his serviette and dabbed his lips.

"It seems that there is nothing left to discuss. You have robbed me of this opportunity!"

Mrs Brasheur shook her head vigorously. "Oh tush! That is too dramatic even for you Joanna-dear. This circumstance has merely opened up two opportunities. Now *two* people have been engaged in a position. And we are reassured that my cousin has a responsible carer."

"That is not my point. You promised I could apply for the school. All your talk about the temporary appointment of the tutor being about due process was just a way to keep me placated until another permanent teacher could be placed. Your hollow reassurances were never founded on any genuine intentions."

The Reverend shrugged. "Mr Franks is retired, and he generously supported the school as our interim tutor. But we have a permanent teacher now, so there is really no sense in you putting in an application."

"You sent me out to Guthrie's place to get me out of the way! Indeed, you must have been so concerned my application would be very suitable that you needed me to be removed. Far be it from me to interfere with your intention to place someone else, anyone else, in the school. This! Even after you told me that I have every credential needed for the role. In fact, I guarantee I meet every qualification twice over Mr Thomas."

"You have no basis on which to make such an unreasonable claim. The engagement process has been conducted on merit alone. He is an excellent candidate."

"I make that observation based on his own disclosures regarding his schooling and inexperience. It is not a blind claim!"

"It has worked out for the best. We have Mr Thomas as the teacher now."

"What you have is a teacher who will never challenge anything you say."

"This is what is best for the school. And this is what is best for my wife's relative."

"What is best? Oh, I understand perfectly. I understand it is best that I do not go back out there. You have sabotaged the possibility of them obtaining an experienced nurse. You have sabotaged my dream of attaining a position as a teacher. I came all the way here, on *your* recommendation to my aunt." A cold breeze blew in under the door and the lamps in the room flickered wanly.

The Reverend scowled. "Be careful, Miss Grenham: *'Pride goeth before destruction, and a haughty spirit before a fall'.*"

"This is not pride. I have always been very frank with you about my hopes. You know I only came here because of the school, to be engaged as your teacher."

"I trust you understand we cannot continue to extend charity for you to reside here. Especially since, as a fatherless spinster, your prospects are grim. If you are unwilling to take a perfectly suitable position at our cousin's domicile, it will certainly void the arrangement we made with your aunt. *'If any would not work, neither should he eat'.*"

"I haven't been staying here on charity. I have been paying board. Generous keep. But if you insist on the concept, whatever happened to Christian charity beginning at home?"

"If you refuse to work in a perfectly adequate position it would be best if you elect to go somewhere else to reside. At least until you find leave towards other employment."

"Are you forcing my hand? There is nowhere else. I have waited and waited for this opportunity. And what about the Guthries? They will never find another placement out there without your help."

"I am glad you understand. We are helping."

⁂

Joanna put on her overcoat and scarf. She went for a walk along the street, her gloved hands pushed deep into her pockets. The cold night air seemed to bite as she breathed in. Gradually the lights in the windows of the houses went out as their occupants turned in for the night. She watched the moon rise yellow over the hills, and then turn to silver in the clear night sky as it glistened against the dew fall. She turned and wandered back to the manse, but rather than going up to her room, she continued to walk through the church yard, up to the church. She knew that if you raised the knob on the half turn, the latch lifted. She pushed open the side door, and walked into the shadows.

She sat on the front pew as the moonlight streamed through the stained-glass window onto the communion table at the altar. Joanna stood up and went and lit a candle. It seemed fitting in a way. To light a candle for something that was so precious to her, and its passing away. She always had such an insatiable desire for learning as a child. Her tutors praised her curiosity and her determination to study. It had become her dream to pass that on, to open up the world to others, just as her tutors did for her. So when her widowed father finally drank himself to death, and their family estate was mostly consumed in paying debts he had incurred... it gave her a practical reason to pursue her love of learning, and find a position as a teacher. That's why she was here. That was the only reason she was here.

That last New Year's Eve, at midnight... when she had sat in the church in her hometown, just like this, it had felt like a dedication. A new year. A new season. She knew God was inviting her forward. Teaching was to be her profession... her sacred call, just as others might respond to a call to the priesthood, or to nursing... or to motherhood. Her call was to slate-boards and chalk dust, readers and spelling-bees. She had been so confident when her Aunt had sought out Reverend Brasheur for a referral, and he had responded with news of their own vacancy at their school, that this was her open door. But now that door slammed shut, and she wondered if she had imagined the whole thing. Why would God lure her out into this place in the middle of nowhere, to have her dream, their dream... the dream that her and God had shared in that moment, be smashed on the whim of bigoted, small-minded people? Why would God take this dream away now? Joanna stared at the flickering candle. The flame seemed so fragile against the cold and the dark. Joanna closed her eyes, and saw the imprint of light on her lids... not the dark. That gave her hope. If teaching really was their dream... the dream that her and God shared, then he would not be taking it away from her... but he would be holding it for her. Just because it didn't look like what she had anticipated, didn't make it any the less real. Didn't God share with Abraham in the Bible the dream that he would be the father of nations?

And that didn't look at all like what he thought. Just one child in his old age. Could she also trust God's wisdom that this dream was protected? Perhaps it would be teaching Bonnie. Perhaps that is what he had meant. Perhaps her dream would be teaching one child in an isolated hut, far away from chalkboards and library books. If she did that well, who could tell what impact those ripples would have on the future?

She stood up, and went over and blew out the candle. There was nothing to mourn here now. No death of a dream. Actually, the dream lived on... even if it was a little deformed and a little different to what she had thought. All that was left was just the reality of getting on and doing the next thing that came her way. And her heart sank in the realisation that the next thing was in the shape of a bleak cottage that didn't keep out the cold.

∞∽§∂C₰∽∩

4.

Joanna stepped down from the seat on the cart. She closed her eyes to the dreariness of the hut and the biting evening wind howling around the trees. The driver helped her unload her suitcase, trunk and a couple of boxes. This was the sum of her life. Pathetic. She looked up. Tuck and Bonnie came running out to meet her. "Miss Grenham! You are back! This is wonderful!"

Wonderful was not what she called it. She swallowed back her tears. Joanna gave her a wave and then toppled unsteadily as the dog jumped up, smearing mud on her skirt. Bonnie bounced forward and enveloped her in an enormous hug. She laughed in spite of herself and picked up Bonnie swinging her around. Seasons. This is what it was. The south wind blowing off the mountains reminded her that this was a season of winter. Her winter. And perhaps it was possible to find moments of warm drinks and bright hearths in the bleakness. She had to look for those. That would get her through... until Spring. Surely with the warmer weather they could find a proper nurse, and then her prospects of securing another placement as a teacher would not be in vain.

Bonnie was definitely a smile-moment. Her wind-blown cheeks were chafed red; her hair a matted mess. As she set her down, Mr Guthrie was standing there, his face unreadable. "You came back."

"Yes, well. Apparently, the appointment of a schoolmaster was more urgent than a skilled carer for your wife. So, I am here for a little longer. I'm sure they will find another replacement for you soon enough. In the meantime, I am here for as long as you need me."

"Are you now?"

"Yes. Evidently I am."

"Bon-Lass, tell your mother we have another for dinner." She ran off excitedly. Mr Guthrie turned to her. "You did not want to come back," he said. It was not a question.

"No disrespect to your wife, Sir, but I had my heart set on teaching at the school. I came here because the Reverend and his wife were looking for a schoolteacher, not a nurse. They kept saying if I offered this support to your family, such an example of Christian charity would be considered favourably on my teacher's application."

"The Reverend is traditional. Teachers should be men and nurses should be women. You don't grow a beard."

"Yes. Well, Mr Thomas is barely old enough to grow whiskers himself. I doubt he has even cut his twelve-year-old molars, and yet somehow *he* managed to secure the appointment."

Irvin considered her and his eyes held a smile as he raised his eyebrows. "Did he now?"

She took a breath and decided to risk being honest. "Mr Guthrie, I fear that they may not look very hard for another nurse. Adele is very sick. She needs an experienced carer. If you like, we could try and place her in a hospital in a larger centre. I am so sorry, but that is the way of it. If that is unsatisfactory for you, I will leave as soon as you wish. I really don't want to impose my inexperience on you."

"She's not leaving to stay with strangers. Besides, she likes you."

"Yes, however liking me doesn't give her the expertise that I believe she deserves."

"Bon-Lass has missed her lessons. You teach her."

"Oh. Yes. Yes, you are right. We will certainly continue our lessons. But caring for your wife is my first duty. Tutoring Bonnie is my bonus." She smiled. He was offering her hope like a flickering candle, and she appreciated the gesture. "Do you think I make a suitable governess Mr Guthrie?"

"That you do." And he picked up the trunk and took it up to the hut. Joanna followed silently with her suitcase and tried not to think that she was being sucked down a wind-tunnel from which she would never escape.

She opened the door; the hut was already bleak and cold in the evening shadows. Adele looked up and her pale face seemed gaunt in the dim light of the lamp on the table. Joanna went over and took her hand. Her fingers were cold but before she could fetch a rug from the bed, Adele reached up and embraced her with a kiss. "It is good you are back. Very good."

Joanna straightened up. Unexplainable tears stung the back of her eyes. She looked around. It was evident they had tried hard to maintain order in the house, but some things are just beyond possible. Well she was here now. "Bonnie, let's stoke this fire and have a look at dinner. You are cold Adele. Here – use my coat while I get settled in." And she stripped off her jacket and scarf wrapping them around her shoulders, bustling to take control like a ships' coxswain navigating into a harbour.

They sat down at the table, and Mr Guthrie paused and said grace before they ate. Joanna raised her brow, and smiled quietly while Bonnie eagerly updated her on what had happened while she was away, prattling away cheerily. Adele smiled contentedly. Irvin looked at his daughter curiously, as if seeing a metamorphosis in progress, emerging from a chrysalis.

"Bonnie, I have barely been away for a week. You speak as if it has been months."

"Well it has felt like months. I have been practicing my letters and spelling. Mummy is helping me read. I try to do something every day."

That made Joanna smile. "Well, you sound like the perfect scholar. I am pleased you are working so diligently. We will have you reading well in no time. I bought a box of my books, so we will have more to work with."

"Can we do some tonight?"

"No, I think not. I need to unpack and settle in. Tomorrow we can start afresh. Come, dishes now. I have a treat for your mother. I brought some tealeaves with me. They say it is a special blend to support an infirm chest and weak lungs. So, allow your father to spend some time with your mother." She took the kettle off the fire and set a pot of the tea in front of them with a couple of chipped mugs. No fine crystal and dinner china here. Joanna bundled Bonnie over to the basin and they quickly fell back into their pattern of laughing through quizzes and problems. Every so often Joanna glanced up to see Adele and Irvin enjoying their undisturbed moment, talking softly, earnestly, and she thought that picture was worth every tealeaf.

❧❦❧

5.

Irvin came and sat down for breakfast. He ate in silence and when he stood up to leave, he paused and sat back down. "I am going away for a bit."

Joanna's jaw dropped. "Away?"

"I need to show you what to do with the animals while I am gone."

She swallowed. "Animals?"

"Get your coat."

"Oh."

"Bon-Lass help your mother. Miss Grenham will be taking lessons from me this morning."

He was at the door, already pulling on his coat and boots, before Joanna really comprehended what he was saying. Adele touched her elbow and nodded, encouraging her to follow. Joanna grabbed her coat and scarf from the rack and hurried outside. "Mr Guthrie, you can't go away."

"Can't I now? Well I *am* going. For about a fortnight."

"Two weeks! You can't possibly be gone for so long."

"Can't I now?" He kept walking towards the barn.

She followed him flustered. "Sir, I don't care for animals. I have lived in town all my life. This is a ridiculous expectation. If I have to be responsible for animals for such a period, it will jeopardise their wellbeing."

"I know."

"And yet you suppose I will do it? I can't possibly."

"Can't you now? I reckon you can."

"You are not hearing me. I know nothing about animals. Why would you leave? Your wife needs you here. You can't go: not now."

"So you keep saying."

In desperation she stood in front on him barring his way. "There must be someone else who could do this for you. I am not the right person."

"Who? I don't see anyone else. You will do okay."

"I don't think so! When are you planning on going?"

"Tomorrow."

"Tomorrow? Tomorrow! Oh my goodness! Have you lost your mind? You cannot run away from what is happening here. Your wife and your daughter need you. Here!"

"If I was running away, I wouldn't talk about it – I'd just leave."

Now she was desperate. "But why? What could possibly be so urgent that you have to leave tomorrow?"

He looked at her. He wanted to dismiss her and tell her he didn't need to explain anything to her or anyone else. Not too many weeks ago he would have done just that. But he needed her on side. He needed her to stay. "Okay..." He nodded and opened the door to the barn.

"*Okay* you will stay?"

"Okay I will tell you *why.*" He pulled up a couple of small barrels and offered her one. She raised her eyebrows and tentatively sat while he straddled the other.

He took off his hat and ran his hand through his hair and leant forward resting his elbows on his knees. "Doctor Fredricks said that, unless we find a more suitable climate, Adele will not see out the year. I cannot put it off. I have to go and find such a place." It sounded as if he believed he could order a warmer, dryer climate like one would order a haunch of meat from the butcher. "I was waiting for you to come back so I could go. It is good you are back. Adele trusts you. But just so we are clear: I am not running away. I need to do this, and I need you to do what you can while I am gone. That is it."

"Where will you go?"

"I have contacts: a mate is working up on Blackstone Station. I'll go and see what is around up there. I'll organise something and we'll move as soon as I get back. Like I said, I can't put it off. Adele has been telling me for years that she will get used to the weather but all its done is rust her away like an old tin can. I should have gone before. But I didn't think it would get this bad. I need your help... animals and all."

Joanna blinked. That was quite a speech. She nodded; her eyes wide. "I'm not sure I can do this."

"You can. You are strong and smart and resourceful. I'll be gone a few weeks. That's all."

"One fortnight has now become a few weeks. It will be a *month* before you are back."

"Probably."

She quickly stood up, grabbed a bucket and was sick. She wavered and quickly sat down again. He held her steady by the shoulder and she felt his strength keeping her firm. She realised then that he was the first person who didn't demean her capacity based on being a woman. He sincerely needed her to do this, even if she wasn't the best option, and even if he was jammed into a corner. She decided she would prove him right. Strong and smart and resourceful. Yes, she would do her best.

"But what if your animals die?"

"I'm taking one of the mules, but I'll leave Hur here. Get him and drag the carcass out into the back paddock. You won't want it rotting close to the hut."

"Oh." Well, that wasn't quite the answer she expected. She took a deep breath. "Okay then. Show me what I need to do."

⁂

6.

Joanna stamped the mud off her boots and came inside. She peeled off her wet socks and slipped on her house shoes, shaking the rain off her coat, hanging it over the back of a chair in front of the stove to dry. She rubbed her hands together over the coals, trying to thaw the numbness. She put on another log and stirred the pot. It was almost pointless counting the days, but it helped her focus. She had to keep going. She had to get through. Surely the sun would shine soon. She turned to Bonnie who was coughing, and she quietly reminded her to use her kerchief. Bonnie's hair was braided and tidy, and she had already set the table. Under the supervision of Adele, she had even cooked dinner.

Joanna smiled. "We are quite the trio of resilient and relentless women. Strong and smart and resourceful. Another day... no dead animals to report. We are doing well." She stood as if presenting a speech for some elegant tea-party. "Congratulations to my beloved companions. Mr Guthrie will be delighted to see his family doing so well." Adele smiled and gave a flutter of applause. Joanna curtsied to Bonnie who returned a faltering bow. "Very ladylike Miss Bonnie. Would you like to dance after our elegant supper?"

Bonnie giggled at the game and her eyes went wide. She tentatively glanced at her mother who nodded. "Oh yes... but I don't know any steps. And we don't have music."

"Well, young ladies are never too young to start to learn dance steps. And we can make our own music. It would be my pleasure to provide a rudimentary lesson. But let's eat first. We have had a big day."

They sat at the table and held hands as they said grace. Always they prayed for safe passage and a favourable outcome on Mr Guthrie's mission. They continued their routine of reviewing their day... a highlight, a challenge and smile. It became a game of trowelling through the mud of drudgery to find those shining moments. A sparrow perched on the window-sill with his feathers puffed out in the fog; a rainbow in the clouds after a half-hearted attempt from the sun to squeeze through the raindrops; a nudge from the heifer in the barn as she was given her daily ration of straw; the cat rubbing her warm coat against Adele's legs; the clear taste of rain-water fresh from the clouds. And they smiled and praised each other's celebratory observations.

Bonnie and Joanna quickly washed up the dishes so they could commence their dance lesson. Joanna showed her how to stand; explained the waltz step and the beat. She sang the tune as a count, one-two-three, one-two-three, and stepped her through the dance. As they stopped, they gave each other a genteel clap of approval. "Oh you are a perfect student. This is a great accomplishment. Let us practice every evening, shall we? It's time to read something to your mother before you retire. You choose..."

They sat together as Joanna patiently coached Bonnie through the chosen piece. And then Bonnie yawned and bundled herself into bed, and Joanna helped Adele retire. Afterwards she sat for a moment and made a cup of tea. She felt exhausted and frayed. The energy it required to always be strong, always be positive, always be optimistic. She didn't know how she could do this indefinitely. Just once, she wanted to be honest, and to cry and be scared and to say that she didn't know if Irvin would ever come riding his mule back along the track with news of a brighter, warmer, healthier home. She felt a tear start to fall, but she quickly brushed it aside. She feared if she allowed it, an unstoppable flood would drown her inside like the rainclouds outside. She opened her bible and read a psalm, allowing the words thaw her stiff joints. Had she ever worked so hard? She poured some water into a basin and washed before she retired to her bunk. Tomorrow would be more of the same.

⁂

It hardly seemed any time at all when the dull overcast light of morning filtered into the hut. Joanna dragged herself out of her bunk and stirred the coals and lit the fire. She made a cup of tea as she heard Adele's coughing start again. She had been restless during the night listening to her frequent hacking rattle. Bonnie was coughing at night now as well. The persistent drizzle had to let up. It was like the whole world would never dry out. If it wasn't showery, there was a heavy fog that overlaid everything with fine mist. Irvin had left plenty of cut wood in the barn, but it seemed that they were burning through it at a great rate. She just wanted a sign: a sign it was going to be okay; that Adele would recover; that Irvin would return with good news; that Bonnie would regain her strength. Sometimes she felt so afraid she thought she would suffocate.

Almost on cue, the clouds separated, and a strand of sunlight spilt through the window onto the cushion of Adele's chair. Adele saw the sunlight bathe that moment just as she came out from behind her bedroom curtain. She smiled. "See. It is a foretoken of grace. It is certainly going to be okay. It has been five weeks. Irvin will be back any day now," she wheezed.

Joanna smiled her relief. "Yes, I think so too. What a pleasure to have some sunshine. Here is your cup of tea while I will see to the chores."

When she walked across to the barn, Tuck stayed faithfully close to her side. The rain had stopped. The sun was fighting with the chilly wind that whipped around the muddy yard with a moan. It was almost like the animals could sense an imminent change of season. Perhaps, just perhaps, Lady Spring was on her way. At least the sunshine seemed to herald the idea that even though Lady Spring hadn't arrived just yet, she was poised around the corner ready to reveal herself.

Maybe it was that impression that gave Joanna the inspiration to let the heifer out into the mule-paddock for a chance to take a fresh pick of grass. The paddocks were brown from the winter frosts, but now there was the faintest tinge of green peeking through. The last fortnight of unrelenting showers had kept the frosts at bay.

She slipped the halter over the heifer's head and led her out into the yard. Irvin had acquired her as a calf from Horsham's good Guernsey cow and she was growing into a good-tempered little beast. Irvin was waiting for her to be old enough to put with the bull, so she would become their designated house-cow. To have fresh milk again would be such a treat. The old cow had gone dry months ago. Joanna understood how precious this heifer was. Adele had explained that raising it from a calf was the only way they could afford a quality-bred milking cow like that. She was friendly and tame... more like a family pet than farm-yard stock. Bonnie even had a pet name for it. Joanna smiled as the heifer gave a little kick as the halter slipped off. "Enjoy your morning frolic and fresh grass. I'll be back later to put you inside the barn, so don't get used to it."

Joanna noticed the afternoon shadows getting cool, and she was finishing some numbers with Bonnie when she suddenly remembered the heifer. She grabbed her coat and pulled on her boots. When she couldn't see her in the paddock she frowned. She had expected to see her by the gate.

Joanna climbed through the rails and walked out into the paddock calling for her. She stopped and looked around. It had not occurred to her to check the fences before she let the heifer out, and she hoped she had not escaped because she didn't know how she could explain that to Adele. She walked further into the paddock, calling out. It was then she heard a low moan. She ran through the wet grass following the mournful, panicked sound. The heifer had slipped down a muddy embankment into a swampy low marsh at the far end of the paddock. She had been floundering but was not able to get out.

With her heart in her mouth, Joanna slid down the bank and waded into the swamp. "Come on. There you go girl... out you come!" she murmured as she tried to tug her forward.   The heifer let out a low moan, and Joanna responded with a groan and waded around behind her and tried to push the heifer up and out. "Please don't be stuck. Please move..." But no matter what Joanna tried, the moans from her trembling frame showed she was caught, deep, obstinately in the muddy mush. Joanna was rattled. She had to get her out! The cold afternoon sun was quickly dipping low behind the hills. If the heifer was not out before night fell, she most certainly would die!

Joanna struggled out of the marsh and lent over gasping deep breaths. She had to think sensibly. Think! Strong and smart and resourceful. That's what Irvin had said. What stupidity! Nonetheless she had to be those things now. Yes, she had to be tough and innovative. She struggled back to the house in her muddy clothes dragging against the ground. She retrieved a bed sheet and hitched the mule in the harness collar. She grabbed a number of ropes from the pegs on the shed wall, wrapped up Bonnie warmly and had her come with her. She positioned the mule at the top of the bank and asked Bonnie to stand with him. She tied one rope around a tree, the other to the harness and then used the sheet to make a sling to go under and around the heifer. The heifer was only small, but the suck of the mud seemed to create a vacuum that would not allow her to budge. She secured the mule again to the tree and then went back to the barn and brought back a barrow of straw, a shovel and a bucket. Also, a lamp. She had no idea what would work. What if Irvin came back now? There was no way he could find his prize heifer drowning in mud without any evidence that she moved heaven and hell to get her out. She tried to shovel the mud, but it was like trying to sweep the ocean, as another wave filled what was taken away. Using the shovel like a wedge to lever the marshy mud away, Joanna then packed straw around the heifer. She repeated that on the other side. The floundering heifer's eyes were spooked, and she was quickly losing her will to fight. That fear mirrored Joanna's own terror. Would there ever be someone to calm her panic? She tied the sling again, twisting the sheet to give it more strength. Then she climbed out again. The light was getting dim, and it started to drizzle rain again. Joanna told Bonnie to go back to the house and make supper for her mother. She lit the lamp and prayed to God for another idea, more strength, more spirit... more anything! She stood beside the mule and moved him forward. "Come on Hur. You can help..." Patiently, he pulled. It seemed like the tension in the sling was taking up. The heifer moaned again, and then suddenly the rope slipped and the make-shift harness gave way. Hur lurched forward and the heifer sunk back. Joanna tethered the mule again, and then waded back out to reposition the sling. Again. Try again. Something. Something must work!

It was then, covered in mud, as the evening light finally extinguished from the sky, and rain started to fall again, that she saw the glow of the lantern come bobbing back again along the track from the house. She called out.

"Bonnie! Go back to the house. I have told you! Do not come out here! You have done all you can. It is too cold!" The lantern kept coming. "Go back Bonnie! You must stay warm! Don't take another step!" By now she was furious in her anxiety. The lantern had bobbed out of sight behind the bank, but she was not fooled. "You are not listening to me! You go back now, or I will give you such a spanking you won't sit down for a week!"

"Will you now? Thinking it will be you who will be so stiff and sore, you won't be moving for a week." The lantern was raised and Irvin's hat, shrouded his face by the brim, dripping with rain. He looked around and took in what lay before him.

"Mr Guthrie! Oh. You're here." And she burst into tears.

He slid down to bank and lifted the lantern high. He looked into her face but said nothing.

She wasn't sure if it was shame or relief. She took some shuddering breaths and tried to calm herself.

"Let's see what you've done here," he said quietly. He tested the knots, and retied one side. "Looks like it should work. I'll hitch up the team: two beasts are better than one." He looked at her in the lantern light. "And if that be the case, both of us should be able to sort this out then."

She'd never heard him try to crack a joke before. She nodded and swiped her wet hair from her face, smearing more mud along her forehead and neck.

He positioned the mules, hitching them together: talking and soothing them. He held out his hand and grabbed her by the wrist, pulling her up. "When I give the word, you move the team forward... slow and steady." Then he went back to the heifer and packing more straw around her. "Pull!" Joanna edged the harnessed mules forward and he adjusted the sling, positioned under her haunches, lifting the heifer out. "Stop! Back-back. Allow some slack: the sling is slipping. Okay... now: pull!" Edging forward, regulated by Irvin's instructions, the heifer gained her footing and emerged her frame trembling from cold, stress and fatigue. Irvin put on her halter and led her back along the firmer ground, around to where Joanna was standing, shivering in the rain. He handed her the rope. "Take her back to the barn. Rub her down with straw and I will bring the team back. Right behind you."

Joanna had washed the heifer down and was drying her with tussocks of hay when the barn door opened, and Irvin led his mules in. Her lips were blue, and she was trembling all over. He went over to Joanna and firmly took the hay from her hand. "I've got this. You draw yourself a bath. Go now. Hot as you can stand it. And leave the water in the tub... I'll use it when you are done."

"But Mr Gu..."

"Go now. You did well." He didn't add, as he was looking at the state of his heifer, that he didn't expect she would be still standing in the morning.

♁⊱⊰⊱⊰♁

7.

Joanna stood near the door and peeled off her boots. Bonnie flew out of her bunk and ran over to her, feverish with questions about Ticka her heifer. She quietly reassured Bonnie that her Papa had saved the day, and the heifer. Adele came and helped her out of her layers of mud-drenched clothes and tossed them in an empty wooden half-barrel by the door. They had already pulled out the bath-tub and Bonnie had helped fill it with water. There were large pots of water heating over the fire. Adele had put some gum-leaves in the heating water and the eucalyptus smell filtered through the hut. Bonnie had already had her bath and climbed back into bed.

"How is the heifer?" Adele said, wheezing with a furrowed brow. The exertion of drawing the bath was ignored in the face of the safe return of her husband and the precarious fate of their beast.

"We got her out. He said..." She couldn't exactly remember what Irvin had said. She shrugged, and sneezed.

Adele pointed to the bath. "In the tub now." Joanna stripped off the last of her muddy underwear, rinsed shivering in a low metal wash tub and stepped into the larger hip-bath. The heat stung her numb skin as she ladled the water over her body and it slowly began to permeate her with warmth. She scrubbed the mud from her face and hands and arms, and then lathered the mud out of her hair and doused clean water over her to rinse off. She sat for a moment soaking away the aches. Suddenly she sat up flustered. What if he walked in? She quickly did a final rinse off, ladling clean warm water over her. She grabbed a towel and disappeared behind her curtained booth to get dressed. She emerged, dressed warmly and made herself a cup of tea sitting at the table with Adele, trying a little of Bonnie's stew. She didn't feel hungry. Every fibre of her body was throbbing with exhaustion. Not long after she excused herself and went to bed. She lay there exhausted, unable to relax, unable to doze off. She was stiff and cold as the frozen air seeped back into her bones. She heard Irvin knock on the outside door and she rolled over to face the wall. Tears washed her pillow as their muted talk was intermittently punctuated with coughing, a chuckle and the splash of bathwater. When she did finally succumb to sleep, Joanna finally submitted to the conviction that she had done her time. She couldn't do this anymore. She would go back to her sister's home. Her little foray into independence and social contribution was over. She hadn't expected this.

❧⬧❦⬧❧

Joanna woke disorientated. She wasn't sure what was different. The light was wrong. So was the silence. No coughing. She got up and peaked through the crack in the curtain to their bedroom. Adele and Irvin's bed was already made and the breakfast dishes were washed. Well, clearly everyone was up and about; she had slept in. Then she realised that the rain had stopped, and the sky was clear. She looked outside and saw Bonnie disappear into the barn with Tuck. Then she remembered. She remembered last night. She remembered how she had jeopardised their cherished heifer. She remembered the relentless sucking feeling of mud and rain dragging against her clothes. She remembered her fear. She remembered screeching at Bonnie. She remembered her relief and elation at seeing Irvin... Mr Guthrie... appearing above the embankment like an angel with a lamp. Then she remembered her resolution to leave... and why. She poured herself a cup of tea. Her head ached. Her body ached and was feverish. She just wanted to lie down and sleep for a very long time. She sat at the table and felt the tears again. She put down her cup and brushed her hair out of her eyes. She tied it up before she pulled on her boots and made her way over to the barn.

She wanted to find out, after all that, whether the heifer had made it through the night. Bonnie called the heifer Ticka. She said it was a name that went with Tuck. She smiled as she pictured Bonnie hugging her Ticka as they fed her hay, singing a little rhyme she had made up:

"Tuck and Ticka. Ticka and Tuck.
Having you both is my very best luck.
Tuck and Ticka. Ticka and Tuck".

Joanna pushed open the barn door and realised why she only ever referred to Ticka has 'the heifer'. She had refused to call her by a pet name. Just like she only ever referred to Mr Guthrie by his official designation. Otherwise it was too personal. She knew she was becoming too attached. She knew she had to leave. Anyway, after such a serious error, they would demand she leave. She was sure of that.

Joanna jolted as she saw Adele sitting on a barrel seated beside Irvin... Mr Guthrie. He had his arm around her waist. They were both leaning over Ticka. She gasped at a shooting pain in her chest. Tears stung her eyes. She sneezed.

Adele turned as she come in and looked up smiling. "Good afternoon."

Joanna nodded hesitantly, and sneezed again.

Bonnie bounced up and ran over to her. "She's going to make it Miss Joanna. You saved Ticka's life."

"I should not have let her out. This would never have happened," she said severely.

Irvin straightened up and considered her. "Did you hunt her into the marsh then?"

"No, no of course not! I thought she would like some fresh grass since she didn't seem to be eating the straw. The rain had stopped, and I thought..."

"Then I'm thinking you didn't mean it to happen, but when it did, you tried all you could to see it fixed."

She stood there amazed. "You're not angry?"

He smirked, and affectionately smiled at Adele and put his hand on his wife's shoulder. "I'm mad as hell."

"Oh. Well. That is good news." And she sneezed again and ducked her head to hide her blush.

"Yes. There is more good news: we have a place! Up near Gumleigh Station; past Blackstone way. It is everything the Doctor ordered. Climate warm. Drier than here. Permanent water. The cottage has three rooms; front verandah with a view. The land is perfect for farming. We are going to wind up here... and we are on our way!"

"Oh." She had already resolved on her plan to leave. This fitted exactly with what she had decided she needed to do. But when it came down to it, she felt herself resisting. Well, now she had no choice. She had to leave as well. "How long will that take do you think? Before you go?"

"I'm going over to see Mr Horsham shortly. We talked before I left, and he was keen to add this place to his block. It's just a matter of finalising this sale and that one. It will take a bit of juggling, but we'll leave as soon as we can."

Adele beamed in between her coughing. Even the musty air and the mouldy straw of the barn could not dampen their optimism. Joanna nodded, curtsied and wiped her flushed forehead. "Oh. Umm... I... offer my congratulations. I am feeling quite unwell. I fear these weeks have taken their toll. I will retire if that is agreeable?"

Adele frowned in concern and nodded with a cough. "Of course."

Joanna turned and fled.

Irvin watched her go, shrugged and went back to describing all the advantages of every aspect of their new endeavour.

Joanna collapsed on the bed and pulled the covers up close to her chin. She shivered with fever and this time she did not pretend. This time she did feel weak. This time she cried and cried and cried. All the pressure from the last month exploded feverishly onto her pillow.

⚜

8.

The warmer weather seemed to create a solid sense of hope in every sunray that split the atmosphere. Adele helped with household chores and felt strong enough to venture outside. So, they would go together, picnic pail in hand, to find which ever paddock Irvin was tidying up before the move. They would sit while Bonnie practiced her reading and then they would down books and enjoy their lunch together. Joanna took her art pages and sketched some of those fleeting spring-kissed moments. The miracle of sunshine had wildflowers blooming. Adele assigned Bonnie the mission of picking a wild springtime nosegay. The flowers were put in a preserve jar at home as if they were hothouse blooms arranged in the finest crystal vase. Joanna had a number of still-life studies in her sketch folder of Bonnie's wildflower bush posies.

Adele and Joanna started packing up in preparation of the move. Irvin was negotiating with Mr Horsham regarding the sale of the property and equipment. Even though he believed the farm chattels were worth much more than was offered, he agreed with Adele just to roll with it so they wouldn't get bogged down in negotiations. Everything was directed towards relocating as soon as possible.

They sat around the table, and Irvin lifted his mug. "Here's to new beginnings." There was laughter and chatter as they talked about the move. The anticipation was heady. Joanna nodded quietly and raised her cup too.

Suddenly Bonnie stopped. "Miss Joanna, you are coming with us, aren't you?"

"Oh I... ahh," Joanna quickly glanced towards Adele who sat with flushed cheeks looking at Irvin. "I could visit perhaps. I have made arrangements to go back to the town where I grew up. My sister is there." She swallowed as she noticed she couldn't call that place home. Not now.

"But I haven't finished school. You must come."

"There will be other people to teach your lessons. Your parents will find a suitable tutor. Perhaps they will even have a school closer for you to attend."

"But why do we need to find someone else when we have found you?"

"Bonnie, you are strong and smart and resourceful." She swallowed hard. Irvin had declared those same strengths over herself. "You will do fine in your new home. You don't need me now."

"But I *do* need you. Besides, I want you!" And she stood up from the table and flung herself on the bunk muttering about the unfairness of life.

Joanna quickly ducked her head and stood up, clearing the dishes wordlessly. The celebratory atmosphere was crushed, and Adele sat there, sort of stunned. Irvin had put down his fork and flexed his hand while his face contorted in silent frustration. She scraped the plates and added water to the basin.

Adele started wheezing and then coughing again. Joanna automatically put the kettle on to steam and added gum leaves for that bush tang of eucalyptus. She stoked the fire, as the evening air was already cool. This was routine. It was not unusual for the night air to start her again like this. Joanna brought over the steaming bowl and the light cheesecloth cover that Adele would put over her head, and then supported her shoulders as she leant over it. Adele started gasping; every thought, every fibre focused on the next rasping breath.

But this time it didn't abate. The only sound in the hut was her strained wracking breathing. Bonnie had relinquished her bunk, and Adele sat there propped up on thin pillows, her frame trembling every time the coughing took over. Finally, Irvin could stand it no longer and left to get Doctor Fredericks.

When the doctor came in, Joanna had dozed off leaning on the side of the bunk, exhausted, numbed by the rasping of Adele's persistent gasps. Bonnie was asleep on her mother's bed, the pillow wet with her tears. Joanna jolted awake and moved aside for Doctor Fredericks. Adele stirred, her face flushed from a spiking fever, her frame wracking with more coughing as she moved. The Doctor examined her, and signalled Irvin and Joanna to the side and spoke in a low voice. "It is the Catarrh Pneumonia again. Adele's reoccurring bouts are putting excessive strain on her system. I don't know how long she can take this." He took out his bag and called for towels and a bowl and performed a blood-letting.

Irvin left abruptly and went out to the barn. Joanna's mind was swimming with confusion and fatigue, assisting as best she could. "Doctor, I don't understand. She was so much better. The warmer weather was helping. She was doing well. Surely she is not in danger now."

"She is in great danger. And the weather has little to do with these fickle humours. Her constitution is weak from all that she has endured. We do what we can."

"But you advised them to seek out a warmer climate. Now you suggest the weather means nothing?"

He frowned and cleared his throat. "Mrs Guthrie has concurrent asthma and Catarrh Pneumonia. Each condition exposes her again to the other. It is a dangerous and complicated combination. Climate is thought to have some impact on the asthma, but the other comes and goes on a whim. Just because you are her nurse, doesn't mean you understand the complexities of these matters concerning constitutional afflictions." He scowled and Joanna was left staring at the empty doorway as he abruptly left and rode away.

Dawn broke over the little farm hut and daylight showed more clearly just how great the threat was. Adele lay on the bunk frail and drawn. Her skin was tinged with grey as she struggled for every breath.

⁂

Joanna leant over and adjusted the pillows. She pulled the tray closer and positioned a towel. "Some broth Adele. Please..."

She nodded. And tried to take the spoon. Her hand shook and exhaustion tackled her back into the pillows. "Maybe later..."

Joanna's face puckered in distressed. "Oh no Adele. You said *later* before. You must eat something. You have barely had anything for days. Please. Allow me to help. Mister Irvin needs you to be strong. Please! You must try."

Adele lay back on her pillows, pale and serene, and seemed to smile. "I have a favour to ask you Joanna."

"Oh yes Adele... anything. Would you like some tea? I still have some leaves. They do help some."

"This is more... more... more important than tea..." She closed her eyes for a moment. "I want you to look after them... when I'm gone..."

"Hush Adele. You can't talk like that. We are doing everything we can to make it better."

"I'm not senseless. I won't make that trip. You must..."

"Bonnie needs you. I'm sure that if..."

"Irvin. I meant Irvin." Her skin was dry from her fevers, her lips permanently blue around the edges, and her eyes glazed and dull.

"Oh! Adele. I know you mean well, but that is not up to me. Irvin loves you. He won't..." She couldn't even finish the thought. Tears filled her eyes.

"Irvin is practical... always practical. He will do it... because it is obvious."

"It is obvious you are delirious! Hush. You can't talk like this."

"He has noticed you. I don't want you to dismiss it because he is not a talker. Yes, I know Bonnie needs you. But he needs you too. Please. It will make my passing easier to know."

"Oh Ma'am! I can't promise that! It isn't right. You should not lose hope. We must always have faith and hope."

Adele smiled and shook her head. "I know what I know. Promise me..." she whispered faintly. She looked past her across the room and smiled again.

Joanna looked around and expected to see Bonnie or Irvin standing there, and for a moment she was horrified that they might have heard her rambling. The shadows were empty. That was a relief... but at the same time, it spooked her some. "Ma'am! Adele. Please take some broth. It will make you feel stronger."

She seemed to rally. She nodded. "I will try..."

"There. That is better. No more silly talk. We are going to beat this. We have done so before. We are fighters: each one of us. We are not giving up."

~◦৪০C৪~৯

"Irvin...?"

"I'm here."

"Promise me that you will still go. Bonnie... our Bonny girl... I fear she has my lungs ... she needs to be there... where there is sun..."

"We will all go when you are stronger; like we planned. All of us together."

"You are not a coward Irvin Guthrie. You know the truth. As do I. Promise me you will go ahead. It is what we talked of... dreamed of..."

He smiled at her with affection and swallowed hard. "You, boss me even when you are weak enough to snap in two..."

"I love you, Irvin Guthrie. Thank you. Thank you for sharing your heart with me."

"Oh Adele..."

"It is okay..."

"No! No. It's not okay. Nothing is okay." His dry eyes seemed to ache from the depths of his soul.

"But it is okay... it's okay... to love the next person. Don't let your loyalty to me stop you." She coughed, her whole frame trembling. "You do what is right for Bonnie... for you and... Joanna..."

He turned. "Joanna?" He cleared his throat roughly. "Joanna, she is calling for you."

Adele reached out and took his wrist. She wheezed, and he leant down to hear her. "Irvin. You hear me. Do what is right. Don't put it off."

Joanna appeared. Pale and drawn.

"She's calling for you. Take no notice... she is talking nonsense."

"I think she is very lucid Sir. I've have heard her only talk about her love for you and Bonnie..."

"As you say," he said abruptly. And he grabbed his coat and went outside. She heard wood chopping soon after.

Adele smiled and closed her eyes. "He heard me fine."

Joanna adjusted her pillow and offered a drink of tea, holding the cup to her lips.

∼⊱⊰∽

9.

Joanna dared not look at Reverend Brasheur as he clutched his prayer book severely. She could feel his disapproval and was sure he charged her guilty for not executing her responsibilities suitably. It seemed he equated this failure with premeditated murder. Carers were not only to care; they had to perform miracles as well. Bonnie's plain black pinafore was starched, her hair plaited tightly. She held Joanna's hand firmly, steadying herself. They walked silently to the front of the church and laid some wildflowers in the open casket. They stepped back. Irvin had not moved for a long time, standing before the casket in his black suit. Eventually he leaned forward and removed his wedding band. He placed it in her still blanched hand... and wordlessly sat down.

Reverend Brasheur cleared his throat and said a prayer. His wife's face was grim under her veil as she glanced at them sitting together. Her lips were pressed thin and looked as if at any moment she would stand up and rebuke Adele for lying so silently and still, with a firm, "I told you nothing good would come of this!" The Reverend spoke a few words, impatient to commit this body to the ground. The men came forward; Irvin at the front of the procession and they stoically proceeded to the prepared plot outside. Another prayer. Dust to dust; ashes to ashes. The people dispersed solemnly.

Joanna stood there with Bonnie, until the men came to complete the filling in. She turned away, holding Bonnie's hand tightly. It felt so inadequate. For someone so remarkable, so loved, Adele deserved more. Much more. They walked back towards to the church and every so often someone paused to pat Bonnie's head or offer their condolences. Mrs Brasheur was waiting by the cart.

"I need to talk with you Joanna-dear."

"Of course." She squeezed Bonnie's hand before she released it and walked a short distance to the side.

She cleared her throat. "You do understand that we cannot continue to pay carer's support to you now." She spoke in hushed tones.

"I know. I understand that."

"Oh, that this good. I am relieved you understand. You looked like you intended to go back there. We have your room prepared. My husband is insistent. Naturally, we will send for your things in due course."

Joanna looked up at her astounded. "But of course I am going back! I am not deserting a child who has just lost her mother. How insensitive do you think I am?"

Mrs Brasheur's eye's flashed. Her voice dropped even lower. "Don't accuse me of insensitivity Miss Grenham. Adele was my cousin. You are a nobody!"

Huh. How about that? Now the cousin's first name gets used. "I am the nobody who has been with this family for the last six months."

"Let me remind you it was at our expense. For you to go back there now would be unfitting. You need to consider..."

"I have considered it. If you are implying I might in some way compromise my reputation, let me assure you my honour has always been respected there."

"You cannot go. You will be damming yourself for wilful sin."

"My only intention is to..." She stopped. Did she really have to explain herself to these people? God knew her heart. He knew she was there for a short while more, motivated by care and kindness. She knew after Christmas Irvin was moving on with his plan to relocate to their new home. And she was leaving too... in the opposite direction. And what she knew was tearing her apart. She had written to her sister and updated her with the details of her return. She had to move on, just as she had planned. Her breath shuddered as she inhaled deeply. "Well. Your duty is done. You have warned me of my eternal safety. However, Bonnie needs me."

"Her moral welfare is sure Ma'am. I will not be staying in the house. I have made other arrangements." Irvin's voice was quiet and firm.

"You are deserting your child? That hardly seems appropriate given what she has gone through." Mrs Brasheur eyes narrowed under her veil and she lifted her chin.

"So you say. Good day Ma'am."

"Well, I never," she huffed.

She grunted again definitely as Irvin offered Joanna his hand and helped her step up onto the cart bench seat. Then he lifted Bonnie up and went around to the other side and sat beside Joanna. They said nothing all the way home. Joanna put her arm around Bonnie and the silence and the rocking and the emotional depletion of the past harrowing weeks, soon had Bonnie fast asleep.

When they pulled up, Irvin carried Bonnie inside and laid her on her bunk. Joanna took off her bonnet and automatically set the fire to make supper. Irvin went to unharness the mules. When he came back inside, the table was set. She served their meals in a regular routine rhythm without saying anything. He sat, folded his hands and they said grace. After he had eaten for a bit, he put down his spoon. "I'm not sure of a highlight. The challenge is obvious... but we got through it. My smile was when you told that woman you were coming back even though she threatened you with eternal damnation."

Joanna breathed easier, almost out of relief. She had not expected that he would say anything after such a difficult day. "Do you think Adele would have minded that I spoke to her cousin so?" She stopped then. Was she allowed to speak of those passed on? Would he despise her for that?

He nodded unfazed. "I think she was applauding you. That woman has always treated us with snobbery. Welcome to the family," he said with a wry smile.

"Thank you for reassuring her concerns. That was quick thinking."

"Oh. That." He took a long drink from his mug and set it down. "I wasn't just talking. I *have* made other arrangements."

"You are going?" Something like panic filled her chest. She put down her cup. She quickly glanced over to Bonnie tossing on her bunk and spoke fiercely through clenched teeth. "You can't go!" she said muffling her volume so as not to disturb Bonnie.

"You spend a lot of time telling me what I can't do, Miss Grenham."

"But I mean it... you can't. You really can't."

"In truth, I'll not be staying here. I'm not sleeping in Adele's bed, our bed... not now. I won't."

"Oh yes you can. You must. Especially now. Bonnie needs you." *I need you*, she screamed silently inside her head

"Bonnie will be fine. You are here. And if not, she can come and sleep with me in the shed."

"The shed? Oh. As in... the barn?"

He nodded into his bowl and ate more of his stew without looking up. "One and the same."

"Oh. Oh." She took a sip of her tea, trying to calm the burning in her throat. "Oh. Well that is appropriate, I guess."

"Glad to have your approval." He finished his plate and stood up. "Will see you for breakfast." And he went into the bedroom and jolted as he saw the mattress stripped bare. He closed his eyes, changed out of his suit and threw it on the bed. He pulled on his work clothes and boots and left without a word.

⁂

Bonnie woke in the night whimpering. Joanna came out to her and sat beside her bunk. "Miss Joanna I can't sleep..."

"Me neither..." Joanna brought her into her bed, and tucked the woollen blanket pieced together by her mother, around her shoulders. "Let's just lie here for a bit then..."

Bonnie sniffled as tears rolled down her face. "I made Mummy sick."

"Oh no Honey, it is not your fault. Your mother was unwell for a long time. We all tried to help her. I don't understand why it didn't work. But Bonnie, she would never want you to blame yourself for her being sick."

"But I wanted you to stay... and then she didn't get better. I was very naughty to want that."

"Bonnie... liking me doesn't stop you loving your mother. Perhaps there is room for all kinds of love in our lives."

"Mummy liked you."

"And me her."

She coughed some, and then quietly whimpered. "Can I stay in your bed? I don't want to sleep in my bed. Perhaps I would die there too."

"Oh Honey. Just because you sleep in the bunk does not mean you will get sick too. Here, how about we swap? You can sleep in your old bed and I'll sleep in the bunk?" She felt like Irvin. She didn't want to sleep there either.

"Miss Joanna? Please don't go..." and it was not just the plea for a night vigil.

Joanna could hear the echo of her thoughts through the voice of a nine-year-old. What did the Bible say: "...*out of the mouth of babes*"?

"Snuggle here then; we can both try to sleep now."

∿₧₧₧₧

They developed a strange sort of intermediary routine. Joanna doggedly insisted that Bonnie continue with her lessons, however shortened and modified to accommodate the grief of a family. She made every effort to keep the meals coming and the housework up to date. And always there was an insistent commentary from Bonnie who wanted Joanna to commit to travelling with them.

Irvin quietly resumed the negotiations regarding the sale of the property that were put on hold with Adele's illness. He went back to Gumleigh for a few days to finalise the purchase and when he returned, he confirmed the time of their moving was set for just after Christmas. When Joanna heard this, she felt the wind being knocked out of her. She wanted to plead that he change his mind or his timeline, but she no grounds on which to make such demands. Of course they had to leave. Of course. Adele was right. The plan must prevail. It was better for them; better for Bonnie.

~ೞ೧ೣ~

Joanna walked with Bonnie out along the track. The glare of the sundried paddocks made her adjust her bonnet. They were talking together about some of the memories of this place, special moments that Bonnie could pack up and take with her. Joanna was determined that she would help her remember not just the pain and the loss and dreariness. They turned and were heading back to the hut when Irvin joined them. He jumped off his mule, leading him by the reigns as they were walking together. "Bon-Lass, jump up and take Aaron back to the barn, will ye?" Bonnie quickly looked at her father and without a word of objection allowed him to hoist her up and jogged off down the track.

Joanna looked at Irvin walking beside her. He awkwardly took off his hat and held it in his hands. She didn't quite know what to make of that.

"I wanted to thank you. For taking care of Bonnie. It is hard on her... adjusting."

"Hmm. I promised Mrs Brasheur of my duty. This is hard on everyone. Even you..."

"Me?"

"Yes, you." She reached out and touched his arm. "You cannot be senseless to this loss. She was your wife."

He stopped and stared at her fingers on his arm as if they were in some way not connected to the rest of her standing there. He didn't take his eyes off her hand. "Not senseless. No."

She looked up into his face. "So how are you fairing then? Are you okay? Irvin... I want so much to help your family... help you... through this time, but I don't know how to start."

Irvin swallowed and looked straight ahead. "I'm grateful for what you are doing... for Bonnie," he repeated.

Just Bonnie? "Oh. Okay." She removed her hand and sighed. He plainly didn't want to talk about this... or him... or them. Perhaps there was no 'them'. She had thought perhaps... hoped... that Adele might have been on to something.

He eventually cleared his throat as they resumed walking along the track. "I'm going to check some stock over in the side paddock. I'll be back later for dinner."

Joanna stood and watched as he strode away into the cover of a clump of trees. This is how it was. Just when it seemed like she was getting close to connecting. Or close to the truth of how he was really faring... he ran away. Disappeared. Either in person, like he was now, running off to deal with some non-pressing job urgently... or he'd emotionally disappear behind a façade of tough coping. He was a man silently retreating into his grief. He kept his distance and wouldn't let her comfort him. She was shut out.

Still, at least she was here. Something within her heart wanted this in-between sort of life to become her normal all-the-time life. It was an impossible aspiration though. He could not even sleep in the bed he shared with Adele. It was becoming clearer to her that Irvin Guthrie would never accommodate another wife after the loss of his love.

⁂

10.

One morning Bonnie woke and said with an air of determination, "I need to see Papa." And she flew out of bed and ran over to the barn still in her nightgown.

Joanna was less flamboyant in the mornings. She felt trampled and drained. Even with the warm weather, as the calendar got closer to Christmas, she felt flatter and thinner: two-dimensional. It was like these people had given her a third dimension of depth that was so unexpected, and now it was being scraped away. "We are not fancy people here," Irvin said over and over. That mantra had not changed from the time she arrived. He stayed true to that declaration. But the simplicity that this family had introduced to her, the kindness and love through the straightforward plainness of their manner, had touched the very core of her soul. It endured through the toughness of their life, and the hardness of the tragedy that knocked on their door, and hijacked their love.

She walked over to the barn, silently wondering how she could declare her willingness to go with them, if only he would be open to it. "Obvious..." Adele had said. Part of her rebelled against the notion of just being the blatantly practical option. She desired to be preferred, chosen, wanted. She slipped through the door that was ajar and heard Bonnie making a case for Joanna joining them.

"Bon-Lass, you don't understand…"

"But I do Papa: I do. She has to come with us."

"No she doesn't.   She can't."   He sounded very irritated. "She is a fancy one. You just have to get used to the idea that fancy is something that I would not be comfortable with…"

Joanna quickly retreated. She didn't want to interrupt any more of Bonnie's defence that was falling on his deaf ears, and her broken heart. Well at least she now knew without any doubt. She hurried back to the hut and started scrubbing the table, getting ready for breakfast. So much for fancy. She resented that her privileged background would exclude her, disqualify her. Even though such a background was completely meaningless now, as Reverend Brasheur repeatedly reminded her: her prospects were now decidedly dim at her age and station. Yet she never pretended to be different to what she was. She wasn't going to adopt coarse manners, just to make Irvin feel comfortable. She had to get through three more weeks. It seemed like an intolerable tunnel that would never end. Christmas couldn't come fast enough.

Irvin turned to his daughter and took a deep breath. He didn't want to trap another woman, refined and of a class that should be out of reach. Look what it had done to Adele. No one deserved that. Not Adele, and not Joanna too. He stared at his daughter's anxious face. She was as persistent as her mother. He sighed, with sadness in his eyes and affectionately hunkered down before her. Adele was right. He loved the next person, and no matter how he rationalised this, it felt like betrayal. "Oh I know Bon-Lass. I know. I want her to come too. I do... but anyone who has only fancy clothes and bonnets travelling all that way would never make the distance. That's not right." Bonnie's face fell and her lips began to quiver. He quickly reached out and hugged her and added in a whisper, "So perhaps if we buy her a practical bonnet... one she could travel in... maybe she might consider it? What do you think?"

Bonnie squealed and jumped up. She returned her father's hug. "I don't think Mummy would be sad. Miss Joanna was her friend. If it had to be someone, she would like us to have our friend with us still."

"Perhaps. But you can't talk to Miss Joanna about this. This is something I need to do. When the time is right. Do you hear me Bon-Lass? You must leave it to me."

"Yes Papa."

He touched her lips. "Promise me Bon-Lass? Shh... Our secret."

"Our secret..." And she pressed her forefinger against his lips. "Shhh..."

Joanna noticed Bonnie no longer harped about her moving with them. She silently acknowledged with a resigned sort of despair, that even Bonnie had got the message that Joanna was not welcome.

⁓ఈౖCౖЖ⁓

Irvin drove the cart over to the barn and Bonnie climbed down. She was tired from the outing into town. He had traded some equipment and finalised the paperwork on the sale. He had brought back some boxes, and other things needed for the move, and set Bonnie the task to help pack up some things in the shed.

Then he set to finishing some wooden cages he was making for a couple of the hens to take with them. His endeavours were more because they were favourites of Bonnie's rather than being irreplaceable poultry. Joanna came over to clarify whether there were some particular household items he had arranged to leave behind and what else she could pack up. As she pushed open the door, he put down the brace and bit he was using and stood there leaning over the bench in his sleeveless shirt.

He said nothing for a while, then he sent Bonnie to fetch him a drink from the house. He cleared his throat awkwardly, blowing some wood shavings and sawdust out of the drilled holes. Now. He would try now. "What do you think we would need to set up house there?" He hoped she would notice the "we" so it would give him a lead in.

Joanna took a deep breath. She didn't want to think about them starting over without her. "I wasn't sure. This is why I came over to ask."

"But if it was you... going out there... what would you take?"

She shrugged. "I don't know."

He looked at her and sighed. "Thinking this is the first time I have seen you without an opinion."

"Well this is different isn't it? What I might take would be different to what you and Bonnie may be comfortable with. It is not up to me to make those decisions for you."

"I like the way you keep house. Would be a fair place to start."

"But there is such limited space on the wagon. There are practical things for the farm and house that need to go, but there are also sentimental things that belonged to Adele. This is an impossible decision for me to make on your behalf."

"I'm not sentimental." Huh. Maybe he was. He was hanging on pretty tight. That thought made him frown. "Are you encouraging sentimentality in my daughter?"

"I'm saying I think it is important to have some things that will remind her of special moments and memories she shared. It is the most significant relationship Bonnie will ever have – with her mother."

"Bonnie is a tough kid." Tougher than himself it seemed. It was all sorted in her head. His heart never felt such a mess. Right now, he felt out of his depth. "It is not the only significant relationship she will ever have."

"You need not fear. You will not be displaced by a mother's love. A father's bond is just as important for a daughter."

He considered her for a moment. He had intended to suggest that her own relationship with his daughter was significant, but she seemed determined to deliberately avoid the implication. He hadn't thought he was being obscure. "What about you?"

She shrugged. "Me? Perhaps I see what you and Bonnie have and I wish my own father had been a little more like that growing up. Parents who adore their children are not everyone's privilege." He adored his daughter. She knew that. He adored Adele. He had. So much. He had great capacity for affection and yet knowing that just fed a deep-seated jealousy that he wouldn't, couldn't love her too. Why were her 'fancy ways' so incompatible?

He noticed that she avoided the suggestion with skill again. When it came to talking, he would never win with this one. He had hoped that she would not make it hard. He had hoped she wanted this too. There was no choice but to go with it. "What will help Bonnie remember her mother well then?"

"Isn't that for you and Bonnie to decide? Why are you asking this of me? I don't think this is a fair expectation!"

He looked at her bewildered. Now she had gone from formal to remote to straight out irritated. "Well leave the packing then. I'll sort it when I get in." He turned back to his workbench and picked up his drill and brace. He resumed drilling holes along the other side of the board.

He felt her anger rise against him. Was it his fault his wife died? Surely, she did not blame him? He had not considered that she disapproved of him like the snooty cousins at the manse. She had come from there, but she had stayed here. She even came back. Twice. She held Adele as a dear friend. He had sensed she was different... even with her fancy clothes and ways... but perhaps he had it wrong. Perhaps she was here now only as Bonnie's governess, now that being a carer was no longer needed. Oh but it was. He needed her care. He really did. Perhaps it was just his loneliness and vanity that wanted to believe she regarded him well. His knuckles turned white as he restrained himself from taking her in his arms. His jawline pulsed as he reminded himself again that she was not his. There was no understanding. But plenty of misunderstanding. He determined again to keep this proper. He wished... Oh he wished. He slammed down the block of wood in his hand and stepped back into the recesses of detached and distant. But this time she pursued him there.

"How can you be so dismissive? This is important."

"Well, I thought so. I was hoping for another's opinion on the matter, but you don't seem inclined. So, like I said, you can leave it to us. Me and Bonnie will work it out."

"You are impossible! I came to offer to help. Now suddenly this is my fault?"

"Not blaming you. We will work it out."

"Of course you will. You always do. You don't need anyone! But your daughter does! So just for your information, regardless of your opinion of me, Irvin Guthrie, I am not leaving Bonnie until after Christmas when you are ready to leave. After that you need never worry about me interfering again!" Exactly as she thought: she was not included. She strode back to the house and heard something slam hard against the wall in the shed, as it rattled into silence behind her. All hope drained away that Adele's less then subtle suggestion was any part of his thinking. Even if Adele thought it was obvious, he obviously didn't think so.

☙❧

11.

Joanna heard him come in, but he didn't look at her as she glanced his way. She was sitting in Adele's chair. A small cypress pine tree stood in the corner decorated with bows of rag; garlands of newspaper chains; seedpods and gumnuts. She had hoped as they set up the bush Christmas tree, it would serve as a symbol of a new routines, new rituals, creating a new normal. But it only served as a distraction for Bonnie. Joanna put aside the book they had been reading together and tried not to waver. Her bags and personal boxes were packed and stood by the door. Joanna swallowed hard. She hated goodbyes generally. She hated this goodbye even more. She hoped her basket of gifts would distract Bonnie from the topic of leaving. She needed this over with.

Bonnie jumped up. "He's here! Did you bring it Papa?" She bounded over to him as he held out a wrapped parcel. Bonnie scooped the gift out of his hand and thrust it into Joanna's arms. "He said I had to wait until he came in. Please open it Miss Joanna."

Irvin stared at the table with only two settings and then at her bags by the door. "Now? You're not staying? Don't you want to eat first? It's Christmas."

She couldn't prolong the torture any longer. She thought if she stayed for Christmas lunch, she might lose her dignity altogether and throw herself at his feet in some sort of humiliating display of... Well, that would never do. She had to go. It was time she took control of herself and went on with the plan. A plan. Any plan. She had to go back to town before she could not leave.

"No. I think I should get along before it is dark. The Reverend and Mrs Brasheur are expecting me." Well, they probably wouldn't lock her outside if she turned up on Christmas Day.

"Papa! I want to do the presents now. Please Papa; Please! I have been waiting all day!"

Joanna dared not look up. She refused to cry. She took a breath as she held on to the gift that Bonnie pressed into her hands, grimly as if it would keep her afloat. The paper was reused and crushed; folded and tied with brown string.

"You wrapped this yourself?"

"No silly. Papa did."

And she shook her head and swallowed again at Bonnie's infectious enthusiasm as she turned the parcel over. "Of course. It is lovely." She tugged at the string and the paper fell off in her hands. There was a bonnet wrapped in a shawl. Hardwearing fabrics. Practical old-fashioned styles. Actually, they were both quite ugly.

"Oh." She felt confused. A frown furrowed across her brow. She didn't know what it meant. Or was this just an example of country fashion gone terribly wrong?

"Do you like them?" asked Bonnie looking at her face eagerly.

"Of course. They will be... useful. Thank you."

"Yes! I knew you would. Papa said you would need them."

"Oh well. Thank you." She really didn't think she needed that much help to look so dreadfully unfashionable. Her brow puckered again, perplexed.

"Don't you like them?"

"I... I will think of you every time I wear them." *I was hoping I would think of you more often than that,* she thought as she tried not to consider specifically how she could add these to her wardrobe.

"You must have them to travel. It is a travel bonnet and shawl," said Bonnie, offering her explanation with a sigh of satisfaction.

"Oh. Yes. Well I do have a long way to go. Thank you. I promise I will wear them when I get on the coach."

"Coach? What? No! No! Tell her Papa. Tell her she must come with *us.* You promised!" Her words tumbled over each other.

Joanna's heart stopped. "Promised?" She flashed a look at him still standing by the door.

He glanced up, a question burning in his eyes. "Please..." he mouthed silently.

Bonnie tugged at her sleeve. "You must! You can't stay behind. Not now."

"We are not fancy people here," he said quietly. His look seared into her soul. It was an invitation, a plea, a declaration... and for a moment all other existence was suspended, and they stood alone in the room.

Joanna took a breath. And another. And another. She felt like he had lifted the lantern high on a dark night in the rain and saved her again. She looked down at the bonnet in her lap. Suddenly she remembered sitting at this man's table holding onto another bonnet like it would save her life. What she held in her hand was transformed into a lifebuoy; pulling her to safety. That was something so completely appealing and inviting. Slowly she placed the bonnet on her head, and tied the ribbons under her chin. She turned to smile at Bonnie's eager face. "Oh well, I am not fancy now. That is for sure."

Irvin offered a wry grin and his shoulders relaxed.

Joanna laughed and tears of relief stung behind her eyes. Suddenly she could breathe again as she pulled Bonnie in for a hug. Try as she might, those tears refused to stay discrete and she swiped at them quickly. Regardless they fell onto the shawl, and she shrugged and used it to dry her face.

After a while she picked up her basket. "I have Christmas presents of my own to give. This one is for you to share with your Papa... a family present. Would you like to open it?" Bonnie glanced at her father, who hadn't moved from the door, still standing there in his coat and hat. He hadn't taken his eyes off her, and he faintly nodded.

Bonnie ripped the paper in a hurry. There was a bundle of shortbread wrapped in a calico cloth. Bonnie squealed and gave her a hug. "This is my favourite! Oh yum! This is the best treat! Papa says his Nanna made the butteriest shortbread in the old country." She pulled out a crumbly biscuit and closed her eyes in delight as she tasted the pastry, licking her fingers of the very last crumbs.

She smiled at her enthusiastic delight. "I cannot take credit for the baking. I know my limitations. But it is nice to have a fancy treat every so often." She glanced shyly at Irvin still standing motionless just inside the door.

His eyes locked in on her gaze. "Fancy is okay... at least on special occasions."

Today did indeed feel like a very special occasion. Joanna reached for her basket and handed Bonnie her present. The edges were neatly folded, and there were little stars drawn all over the paper. "And this one is for you Bonnie."

"Is this just for me? You even made the paper fancy."

"Naturally. Just for you."

Bonnie sat with trembling fingers as she pulled the ribbon and out tumbled a paintbrush and some small pots of coloured paints. There was a folder full of pages of hand-drawn pictures to colour-in: drawings of her mother knitting, resting, smiling, sitting, reading. Other sketches were of the hut, the mules – Aaron and Hur, Tuck and Ticka, the trees, wildflowers... of her father ploughing. "This is to help you to remember your time here. You can start a portfolio of new memories. Some of the pages are blank for you to draw memories of your own."

Bonnie gave her another hug, lingering and heart-felt. "Thank you. Thank you. It is perfect."

"This one is for your Father."

"Oh you must give it yourself. That is the rule."

"Hmm..." She didn't move. "If there is a rule for the gift-giver, then there must also be another rule, that the recipient is to be seated with the others."

Irvin unhurriedly took off his hat and overcoat and hung them on the hook by the door. He came over and slowly sat down, his eyes never leaving her face. He hesitated. He had resolved to be gracious about whatever impractical swanky gift she might offer. He untied the string slowly. Knitted socks. He sighed with relief. He didn't have to pretend about this. This was a good gift. "Useful."

She looked at him then. "Not all gifts have to be useful, but I thought this would work for you."

"It does. Thank you."

"Papa this is your present from me."

He unwrapped a hand knitted scarf. He swallowed. Adele had made this. He knew her work. He draped it around his neck. He felt her nudging him forward: *You hear me Irvin. Do what is right. Don't put it off.* "Well. Who would have thought I would have such a fancy thing? Perhaps this makes me fancy now?" He looked over at Joanna, and their eyes lingered in the moment as he cleared his throat. "Bon-Lass. There is a gift on your mother's bed."

She ran behind the curtain and quickly came back with a small square box. Bonnie removed the wooden lid. Inside, packed in sawdust, was a fine china teacup and saucer. She gasped as she lifted them out, the wood-shavings spilling onto her lap. "Oh Papa! *This* is so fancy! Oh my..."

"It belonged to your mother. She was keeping it for your coming of age. But I thought it might be something to have now... to help you remember her well." He looked significantly at Joanna and swallowed.

Joanna nodded and Bonnie carefully put it on the table. She turned and flung her arms around Joanna, her slight little frame racking with sobs. "Oh Miss Joanna I miss her so much!"

"I know Honey. I know. She was so special, and she will always hold a special place in our hearts. That is her

Christmas gift to us... that we can be together and remember her too."

"Will it always hurt?"

Joanna carefully watched Irvin across Bonnie's shoulder as she held her trembling body until it calmed. She hoped that this would not send him back into the recesses of his grieving. "I don't know... but I know we are here together, and it helps the hurting if we are not alone."

He stroked the scarf around his neck, looked at her soberly and nodded. Joanna gently rocked Bonnie, and sang a Christmas carol, soothing and calming, so aware that this Christmas she had been given a gift greater than any other.

As she finished the song, Irvin stood up. "Well now, let's eat. And set another place Bon-Lass. Miss Grenham, Joanna, will be staying for Christmas lunch." And he pulled out her chair as she sat at their table.

12.

"Are you sure about this? You don't even have a proper wedding gown. This is just as I feared. That man..."

"*That* man is the one I am choosing to marry."

"I cannot understand why. It was the same with Adele. No reason would prevail."

"No, I guess not."

Mrs Brasheur peeked through the curtain of the manse. "Well they have arrived." She came over and pinned a short veil into Joanna's hair. "I guess this will have to do."

"It is more than sufficient. Thank you."

She grunted. Her disapproval was not abating. "Well, let's get this over with. Church is starting."

Joanna smiled at that. "Yes. Let's."

As she walked through the door of the church, Irvin turned towards her. She had witnessed other brides walking down the aisle with lowered eyes under veiled faces, but she walked tall, confidently stepping towards the man at the front and into another life altogether. Together. Bonnie stood beside her father and Joanna handed her the bundle of wildflowers she carried. He lifted the veil and their eyes connected.

Reverend Brasheur cleared his throat and spoke over them, trying to drown out the silent commitment that was binding them together in their gaze. His words seemed superfluous. They spoke out vows. They exchanged two simple wedding bands. They signed the Church Register. They were married. Then they sat side by side, on the hard pew, as the rest of the service proceeded. The sermon seemed particularly drawn-out today.

They had a small get-together with the people of the congregation for lunch after church. A farewell. A few more days... and then they would be leaving. Someone pulled out a squeeze-box, and they danced the bridal waltz in the shade of a tree. Ladies shed tears of goodbye and the men gave them slaps on the back, wishing them well. Bonnie had a dance with her Papa and blushed as another kid quickly took his place when the music paused. Joanna smiled as she watched Bonnie confidently take the lead and guide him through the steps. Then they kissed Bonnie goodbye and left her in the care of the Reverend and Mrs Brasheur, as they returned to the farm for the final pack-up.

The buggy rolled on towards the farm. Joanna found it hard to talk over the rattle of the cart, so they sat in silence in the summer heat and she fanned her face, glad of any respite from the intensity of the sun when it disappeared behind a cloud. The sun was setting as they pulled in beside the hut. Suddenly Joanna felt disorientated and nervous. Some wooden chests were already stacked on the wagon ready for the move. The plan was they would leave the small buggy at the farm and stack the larger flat-bed wagon with what they needed to resource their new life. Once they finished loading, they would collect Bonnie on their way through.

They sat for a moment and looked at the dazzling colours of the sunset blaze across the sky. It was not the comfortable connection of two lovers sharing a gloriously intimate moment. She sat there stiffly, unsure what was expected of her. She felt awkward, and wanted to retreat back to the house, a familiar space even amongst the clutter of packed boxes. But before she could step down Irvin clicked the reigns and continued on towards the barn. He jumped down and came around and offered her his hand. She stood self-consciously by the door while he unhitched the mules in the setting dusk light. Irvin pitched some hay over the gate into the mule yard. When he was done, he came over to her. "Now you have my full attention. Come. Let's go inside." And he opened the door to the shed.

"You're taking me to the barn for our wedding night?"

He stopped and looked at her soberly. "Nah Lass. I'm taking you to my heart." And he swept her off her feet and carried her inside. Tussocks of hay were set around to make a bed. It was covered with fresh linen, and wildflowers decorated a canopy of netting that hung from a hoop suspended from the rafters.

Joanna woke dozily on the bed of hay and it took a moment to realise that Irvin stirred beside her. He reached out to embrace her and she turned sleepily towards him. As they lay face to face her eyes flew wide open. She sat upright and pushed him away. She jolted as a rooster crowed close by, announcing the morning dawn. "Oh my! Oh my. Oh no!" She flew up and fought her way out of the netting and clutching her petticoat to her, standing against a barn post groaning in horror. "What have I done?"

Irvin sat up and tried to clear his head. "Joanna! What's going on?"

She stared at him and quickly struggled into her petticoat. "Oh I shouldn't be here. We will be found. You must go. Mrs Brasheur is right. I am condemned to Hell!"

He held up his hand and pointed to the ring on his finger. "Joanna? We are married. You married me!"

"But you love Adele! You wouldn't. You said you couldn't."

"Why are we talking about this now? You knew what you were getting. You went ahead with the plan. We got married," he said again.

Slowly what he was saying penetrated her fear. "Oh." She took a deep breath in. And another. "Oh," she murmured again. The fog of her dream was lifting. "Oh. I thought... I dreamt that Adele was still... I thought you would never marry me... but we had... Oh."

Irvin got up and pulled on his trousers. He came and stood by her side. "Joanna, Adele told me it was okay to love the next person. I have to take her word on that, because sometimes what I feel... it seems like a betrayal."

"I know. I know. It makes sense to have someone to look after Bonnie. I wanted so much to stay that I went along with it."

He took a deep breath. "I didn't marry you for Bonnie."

"You don't have to pretend; I heard you talking to her." Tears stung her eyes. Suddenly she was no longer able to pretend.

"Heard what? Damn it woman, sometimes you can be so irrational!"

"I heard you talking with Bonnie. You said that you would never accommodate me in your heart. And even though I knew you could never love me because of my 'fancy' background, I wanted to believe that perhaps..."

"Oh. Well..." He sat down on a small barrel and ran his hand through his hair, cut short and tidy for their wedding day. "You are right – you are fancy. Yeah, and I did fight this. Like I said, it feels unfaithful. But Adele knew. And Bonnie was right. But you can't leave... because..." He swallowed and shrugged.

"Because?"

"Because... I married you for me."

"What do you mean?"

"I said, 'I do'. No one made me say it. I meant it."

"But a few weeks before Christmas you were so definite. You stood just here and told Bonnie having me along would never be acceptable. You said you would never be comfortable having me in your life. She stopped talking about me coming along after that."

He shrugged and looked soberly into her eyes. "Hmm. Well. I also told Bonnie that I wouldn't be comfortable with you travelling when you didn't have clothes that would make the distance. You didn't have a bonnet that wasn't fancy."

"Really? You judge me on my wardrobe? That is a fairly flimsy argument since all my 'fancy bonnets' survived the trip to get here."

"We bought the hardest wearing travelling bonnet we could find. Bonnie never questioned it. It gave her confidence you would come with us. She stopped her pestering."

"You told her that to stop her fussing?"

He shrugged. "She can be determined... and it gets on my nerves."

"Oh."

"Joanna, I wanted so much to have you stay with us... me... but I didn't know how to ask that of you. Adele was just like you when she came here. Look what being married to me did to her fancy ways. Look at what it did to her! I tried to stay away from you. To protect you from me. I don't want to be your undoing. I didn't want to expose you to the same risk."

"Oh, Irvin but you forget to factor that I want to be with you. Adele was the same. She never, ever regretted being here with you. You were her strength and her joy. I love the same things she saw in you." Suddenly the weight lifted in her chest and it buzzed lightly around her head like music. She wasn't just the governess with benefits. It was more... just as she dreamed. She turned to him and draped her arms around his neck. "I suppose this means I really have to wear that ridiculously unstylish bonnet now. To prove I am one of the un-fancy sorts."

He shrugged and grinned. "We are not fancy people here."

She stepped back and struck him playfully across the arm. "You're enjoying this!"

He caught her arm and held her. "We might be plain, but I'm thinking that some of your fancy ways are rubbing off on us... on me..." He reached out and tucked a stray strand of hair behind her ear.

"You are looking pretty much the same to me Mr Guthrie."

He didn't let go of her hand but drew her in closer. "What you gave us... Adele and me... those last months, we were dearer to each other than before. That was generous... a gift. We'd got in a rut of not doing anything. Some of it was necessity. Some of it was because we didn't know how to do it differently anymore. You changed that."

"You changed me. I wasn't supposed to fall in love with your family... or with you."

"And yet you would go?"

"How could I stay... feeling like that? That night when you came back and rescued me... when you didn't judge me for my mistake... that is when I decided that I couldn't do this anymore. Adele was so improved. I loved her too."

"She knew you regarded her well."

"It feels like I wanted it; that I wanted her to go. But I didn't. Truly I didn't." She looked up with tears. This was her shameful secret. "She wanted me to promise that I would... you know... but I couldn't. Not then."

He shrugged, his eyes not leaving her face. "Sounds like her."

"But don't you think that is awful? She was asking me to marry her husband."

He shrugged again, unmoved. "She told me to marry her nurse. She wasn't lucid at the end. Crazy talk."

"I wanted her to get better. I didn't want this... but I did want it. How is that even possible?"

"Perhaps... you didn't mean it to happen, but when it did, you tried all you could to see it fixed."

She smiled. "That's the same Guthrie wisdom you offered that night of the Ticka-in-the-bog episode. Ticka has a lot to answer for."

"That night, when I heard you screaming at Bonnie in the dark and saw you up to your petticoats in muck, flopping around in the mud... you didn't look so fancy then." He grinned and turned her face towards him and leaned in. "I've never seen anyone all-in like that. We've had carers before... but they didn't care... not like that."

"The way you work like a slave out in the paddocks... and yet whenever you stepped inside that door with Adele you were so tender. And how you are with Bonnie... I have never seen strength in a man like that," she said quietly.

"And now..." And he leant in closer and kissed her. "Now... just now, I don't have to share you with either of them."

❧◦⊱◦⊰◦❧

13.

Every day the anticipation of their dream was drawing them forward. The discomfort of the rutted wagon trail, the burning heat, the pestering flies during the day and the unrelenting mosquitoes at night faded in the glorious glow of the small attentions that Irvin offered. Joanna sighed contentedly and thought ironically that this was the farthest removed notion of the Honeymoon Tour she fantasied about as a child. And yet, even this gloriously surpassed the romantic destinations that she had heard spoken about as a child, when she wove inconspicuously between the skirts of her mother's gossiping guests in their drawing room. She learnt that if she stayed out of sight and out of the way, she was able to overhear many interesting conversations, even among the men. And then she would retreat to the library and research all the strange places and topics that were spoken of. She wondered what her parents would think if they could see her now... lurching over a sea of endless grassed plains in a wagon pulled by unfashionable mules; wearing her ugly hardwearing travel bonnet to satisfy the whim of a child; sleeping under a canopy of stars in the arms of a strong man who loved her in a way that many women in fashionable circles could never dream of.

The shadows were long over the countryside, and it seemed the last few miles were slowest of all. When they finally saw the cottage sitting on the rise, silhouetted in the dusk light of evening, it was everything that Irvin had described. He let out a sigh; Joanna felt a leap in her heart and Bonnie whooped! And each one thought in their own way that Adele would have loved seeing exactly what lay before them; perhaps even watching and enjoying the moment with them even now.

As they made their way up towards the house a lamplight came on in the window. There were other signs of occupation – clothes draped on the balcony rail; boots and chewed bones by the front steps and a dog ran out from under the verandah stairs, baring its teeth, barking at them making even the patient mules shy. Tuck growled from where he lay at Irvin's feet. Irvin stilled him with a word, jumped down with his crop and stepped forward at the barking dog. He raised his arm and it backed away barking. Irvin bounded up the steps and knocked on the door.

"Yes? What do ya want?" A woman in a plain weave skirt and apron answered the door as if she not heard the ruckus caused by the dog.

"Irvin Guthrie. We brought this place. Kinda confused as to why you are here."

"Jimbo! This is Mr Guffried." She smirked. "He says he owns the place."

"Gu*th*rie. I have a bill of sale."

Jimbo eyed him from inside the door. "Can't see how you could have. We've been here for months now."

"We were delayed. My wife..." He shook his head as if clearing a fog. "The delay is immaterial. You are on my land and I want you to vacate."

"It ain't your land. Belongs to Mr Hobbs. He owns Gumleigh Station, which includes this parcel. This has always been the overseer's house."

"Well, it might have been. Until I bought it from him."

"Like I said: ain't possible. I am head-hand here... me and the Missus... and me family, we have the house." On cue, a toddler screamed, and a baby started crying.

"How long have you been here?"

"Are ya deaf or stupid? A couple of months... like I said." He spoke slowly emphasising his words. He smirked, enjoying Irvin's agitation immensely.

His wife stepped forward impatiently. "He got promoted. Over-seer. Because an important job like his comes with a house. This is our digs."

Irvin walked back to the wagon with a frown shaking his head, and leaned against the wagon where Joanna sat hugging Bonnie. "He says it is leased to them as part of his employment at the Station. We will camp again tonight, and I'll sort it out with Hobbs in the morning. I have all the paperwork."

As he sat by the fire poking the coals with a stick, he felt a cramp start to grow in his belly. Hobbs had been so particular about the contract. At the time it had given Irvin reassurance and confidence; but just now... as this workman produced his lease agreement signed and sealed by witnesses, he started to feel a dark cloud of doubt gather.

Joanna came and sat beside him. "You'll be able to sort it out on the morrow, I am sure."

"Dunno. Something is off. I thought we'd be sitting at our own hearth tonight."

"By tomorrow we can determine when they leave. In no time it will be Tuck barking at the visitors, and Bonnie playing on the swing in the tree."

⁂

Irvin walked in and stared at the man sitting behind his desk. He was tall and solid and had a well-groomed beard with some streaks of grey. He didn't stand up.

"Mr Guthrie. It is a pleasure to see you again. I hope that you are as satisfied as ever with your purchase. I trust you and your wife will enjoy good health here at Gumleigh." He'd already had a report from Jimbo. He said his wife didn't look like she was dying at all. His instincts were right: the sob-story of a dying wife didn't ring true. No, you just don't mess with a Hobbs.

Irvin considered him. Why should he have to explain that Adele would never know what they had bought? He just nodded. "I hope so too. However there seems to be some misunderstanding. There are tenants in the house. Why would you lease my property to your head stockman?"

"Now you are right about that: why would I? That wouldn't be right. I only ever sign leases with my own properties, not someone else's."

Irvin breathed easier. He expected resistance. "So you will inform them of the sale and have them moved on immediately?"

"Well I couldn't possibly."

"You need to. They showed me a lease agreement... signed by yourself and two witnesses."

"Well, since you have confirmed they have a signed lease that makes this legal matter. Sounds like they have every right to be there."

"But you just agreed you don't sign another's property. They need to go."

"I don't know what you are implying Mr Guthrie, but as they have a lease, they can and will stay. I always provide my overseers with a home. It is part of my incumbent duty as a responsible station-owner."

"There is no implication Mr Hobbs. It is now open accusation. You have placed someone in that house intentionally to prevent us taking occupation."

"Mr Guthrie, your southern ways are not making any sense. Why would I let you take occupation of my house when my overseer requires it for his family?"

Irvin was getting redder in the face by the moment. "No reason at all, excepting that I purchased it. I have here the bill of sale; the transfer documents. It is all accounted for."

"Hmm. What are the Portion and Lot Numbers on the deed?"

Irvin read it out.

"Well I can see now exactly where the confusion has come from. Here are the gazetted diagrams on this map. The section with my overseer's domicile has different numbers. Would you care to check?"

"I certainly would!"

Without any hurry and without any hesitation, Mr Hobbs unrolled the map of the district and flattened it out on his desk. "We are here... this is the road east. The parcel concerned is here. What numbers did you say? See, these are different numbers. There, that clears it up. My land. I have that deed. You have obviously purchased a different block Mr Guthrie. You need to check these details when making purchases and before making accusations."

"You showed me this map. But the numbers were identical. I confirmed them."

"Well obviously not. I can't see any evidence of tampering here. These are serious accusations Guthrie."

"They certainly are. You swindler! You gave me a tour of that land. You spoke at length of its advantages."

Hobbs looked at him benignly. "All that hardly seems possible. I know my own land. Why would I need to share those virtues with you when I was never going to sell?"

"But you did!"

"I will have to disagree. You are evidently very confused. I will allow that."

"I am not confused!"

"Then that changes everything, because I don't take lightly to be accused of duplicitous business."

"That's a civil way to frame it, you double-dealing yellow-bellied snake!"

"Now Mr Guthrie. No need to get personal. My records can and will withstand any and all scrutiny."

"This is past personal!"

"It seems to me that, if you had done your homework, you would not be in this position. You need to leave."

"I will get what is mine! I don't care what sort of Big Pin you think you are around here Hobbs. You will not get away with this!"

"Don't threaten me Guthrie. When it comes to this community we look after our own."

~~~~~§◊CЗ◊~~

Irvin rode off in a daze. He dismounted when he got to the camp but went straight down to the creek and took a drink of water running over some rocks. He sat there numb with shock. He was not a reckless man. He had checked all the Parish, Portion, Section and Lot numbers against the map and transfer documents. He had been very particular about it. He had spoken to the officer acting for the Registrar General regarding the history of that particular parcel of land. He had confirmed that it was owned by Hobbs and had even offered that they had heard it was for sale. He had freely given his opinion that it was probably not suitable for acreage farming, but something smaller perhaps like market-gardening might work. Irvin had just dismissed that comment. He had seen the land. He knew soils. It was excellent loam. But now that rather unrelated comment grew his doubt. What if the land's officer had innocently provided information on whatever other block this number had referred to? Was it really possible? Had he been taken for a confidence ruse? Could he fight it? He had avoided the legal trail to expedite the process. He had explained his situation clearly. Surely no one would take advantage of a man whose wife was dying? The sale was necessary to save her life. He shook his head again and scooped up water for another drink. But what if?
~~~~~

Joanna came and sat beside him. She said nothing; sitting, sensing his fear and anger... listening to the water rush over the rocky creek-bed as if it was hurrying to get away, to escape. Something had gone terribly wrong. Eventually she said, "What happened?"

He jolted, coming out of a stupor. "Well. He reckons I signed for a different block... not the one he showed me. I need to work out if he's right. If that's the case it could be anything. I have no idea."

⁂

The guy at the Office stared at him from behind his desk. Irvin showed him the paperwork. He got out his surveyed charts. He confirmed his documentation was not for the place where Hobbs had given him the glowing tour. He showed Irvin on the map the actual portion number. The allotment was smaller. It did include a creek, but he commented that gully was not known to be permanent water, so that was little consolation. He wrote down directions to where it was.

The man took a deep breath. "I think that is all I can do to help you."

"You know this Hobbs?"

He nodded. "I am no legal man, but I'm thinking this is not looking good if it is as you say."

"Is this his style? Would he scam a grieving widower out of his place?"

The man winced, embarrassed that Joanna sat waiting in the chairs lined up along the wall and tried not to look at her.

Joanna stood up. "Sir. When my husband says... well... this land-purchase was put in place to protect his first wife's health. But it came too late. I am his second wife."

"Oh." He shook his head. It was too confusing, and he didn't need to know people's drama. He preferred maps and parcel numbers. Until now he believed they were constant and didn't lie.

⁂

They walked up the hill and stood staring at the map in their hand. It was a mere sketch really, yet there was a peg with a lot number on it partially fixed in the ground, stabilised by a few rocks. Their gaze shifted to the landscape before them. They stood on a rocky knoll, barren and hard. There was a little lean-to shelter: a rough open structure with only three walls. What purpose it served didn't seem clear. Apparently, someone had camped there at some point, evidenced by the remains of a fire-pit surrounded by more rocks. The hill ran down to a narrow little creek bed that had a couple of sparse young willow trees that had been planted at regular intervals and a few callistemons that ran along its course. There were a few straggling gums on the other side of the creek. The block beyond extended into sparse rough pasture... but it would never be soil for cropping.   Irvin knew that.   He knew cropping... only cropping.

Irvin shook his head bewildered and took out the deed once more. He checked the numbers on the map again, the peg and the purchase docket. They all matched. Perhaps he hoped that if he stared long and hard, something would change, but the numbers stayed firm and fixed. A fleeting thought allowed that he was grateful that Adele was not here to see this humiliation. How could he be so naive and stupid? All their savings; all the investment of their years together was completely lost. There was no house, no grass, no trees and there was no water. Nothing. He had bought nothing.

❦

14

"What is this?" Irvin sat sullenly slumped on a stump leaning on his knees, his beard scruffy; his look surly. He held a drawing in his hand. It had been crumpled and smoothed out again.

"It is what you cannot see," Joanna said as she put down his lunch on the barrel beside him.

"And what is that supposed to mean?" His speech was splattered with expletives. Joanna didn't wince. Not now. Not after all this time.

"It means you cannot see what you have; only what you do not have."

"I have tried... tried..." He couldn't finish. He screwed up the paper again and pitched it into the open fire. He watched the ball of paper flare up and turn to ash. "You have no idea!"

"You think I don't know? Do you think I have not been here with you for the last six months? I have been here for every minute of it! Six months of waiting for some sort of resolution to this horror. But what if there is no miracle for us? What if this is all it ever is? Will you stay forever in this state of angry limbo while your daughter grows up watching you waste away on hate? Irvin Guthrie, this is not the man I married!"

"You only married out of pity anyway. Well pity you! Now."

"You think that my decision to marry you was mere 'sympathy'? If that is what you think, *that* is truly pitiful!"

"You can't think this is okay. It will never be okay!" He said it with a growl that rose up from his belly, and he smashed his fist down on the barrel in front of him.

"Whether it is or not, you don't get pity. Not from me. I was never sorry for you. Not then and not now! Ever!"

"Why ever not? This is the worst woeful mess I can imagine. I drag you and my daughter out here with nothing to show for it. If you have no sorry left for me, at least feel sorry for yourself. You made a huge mistake Joanna. You should not have married me."

"I *still* have no sorry for you. Nor for me. We came here for one reason: to get more sunshine. We needed weather that was more suitable for Bonnie. On that criteria alone, Gumleigh has delivered."

"Huh. Small consolation I would say!" The words spat from his mouth.

"Small? It is winter now... and we camp in this open shack with only a hessian wall on one side... and yet Bonnie is not coughing. We have had no nights leaning over a steam bowl with a towel on her head. Not one! Can you seriously forget so quickly?"

He looked at her. A frown creasing his face in a deep scowl. "It ain't right."

"For once I agree. This isn't right. You are strong and healthy. Your wife and your daughter are well and healthy... and yet we cannot enjoy it. That is not right!"

"Enjoy? This can never be enjoyed! It is not right that he gets away with it!"

"I'm not interested in Hobbs! If you want to talk about hate... I hate that man! I hate what he has done! I hate that he has taken my independent, strong, smart and resourceful husband and reduced him to a smear of who he used to be. But what I hate more is that you allowed it!"

"I allowed nothing. This is not my fault. We were robbed blind, and try as I might, he still gets away with it."

"That is just it: you *have* tried! You've given every ounce of energy to this fight. You have tried every possible avenue of recourse. But it is like nothing else will ever happen unless you get just one result. But what if we never get *that* result. Is our life over? Sometimes the story doesn't have a happy ending. Sometimes justice is not served. Sometimes the hero is sacrificed, or dies in battle, or is cheated out of his life savings. Sometimes he has to find the back door into the castle and search out another way to get the treasure."

"You read too many books."

"Perhaps, but just in case this is too subtle for you, the treasure in this story is not some block of green grass with a house on a hill. The treasure has always been us. But you are throwing us away, Irvin!"

"You should have never married me."

"I know Mrs Brasheur would certainly agree with you. But what is done is done."

Letting that self-righteous lot be justified in their accusations didn't sit right with him either. He grunted and looked away.

Joanna pushed in harder. "Do you want to know why I married you? Because I was madly in love. Insanely in love! I was so jealous of what you and Adele had. And then by some horrible twist of fate, I was offered a chance to be part of an impossible dream. I wanted that dream. I wanted you. I wanted you for me. I wanted you to work hard and be strong for me out there, and then to come home and be tender in here... for me. I love you still Irvin Guthrie, but the dream was never the house. The dream was always you."

"So much for all your gullible idiotic notions. They have fallen into the coffers of some untouchable con-man. See I can wax lyrical too; tragedy is poetic as well."

"I have given you six months to sort this, but you haven't found a way. So now it is my turn; with or without the poetry."

"It makes no difference! I can't fight this! No matter what I try, it is like hitting a fortress. You know I have tried!" His eyes turned desperate, silently screaming to be validated by the impossible cliff-face that impeded his progress.

"Exactly! You have done everything. There *is* no way to fight it. That is exactly my point!"

"What point? There is no point."

"Somehow you have to hear this. It is time you knew."

"Time, I knew what? You think that anything you have to tell me could possibly be news? I already know. I know there is no way out. I know I have never felt so angry. I know I have never felt so humiliated. I know I have never been so stuck. All of this – it disgusts me! That's what I know!"

"But not us Irvin. We don't disgust you. Not me. Not your daughter. You don't hate us and yet you behave as if you do. This is not what I want for our baby. Not this!"

"Bonnie is tough enough." He stared at the coals where the remains of the screwed-up drawing stayed in a flimsy wad of grey ash on the edge of the fireplace.

"No. Not Bonnie."

"Bonnie is..." He froze and stared at his mug before him. Eventually he stood up and slowly turned and looked at her. "Hell, that is all we need!" He slammed his mug down and stalked off to the gully.

Joanna watched him pace and eventually sit down by one of the willow saplings, defeated. She turned away, tears streaming down her face, bleeding into the thick lace on her collar. Her dream had become a nightmare. She could not make this Hobbs become ethical. She could not change the numbers on those watertight contracts. She could not make Irvin choose to let it go.

Initially the drawings were an exercise in sanity: to try and see this with different eyes. She used that to buffer Bonnie from the tension and the sullen outbursts over and over. It became their game again, to identify the highlight, the challenge and the smile. Could she find what they did have, rather than what they did not? They had sunshine. They had health. They had stone. She even suspected they had access to underground water.

She experimented sketching different stone huts. She always drew the line of willows in the background. A marker of this place... not some other block of land that was out of reach. This was right here, right within in their grasp. Could Irvin ever see this as potential, rather than a prison? She watched him down by the tree, sullen and withdrawn, and she doubted he could ever make that shift.

⁊⁓⧉⧉⁓⁊

Joanna walked down to the gully and sat beside him. She resisted the urge to berate him again. Irvin ran his hand through his rough hair – a gesture of despair perhaps, or frustration. One cannot get use to the taste of shame and failure. The sun spilt over the red earth and seemed to highlight the ginger tones in his beard. "I'm not given to conceding Joanna. But I didn't see this coming. I failed. You and Bonnie deserve better."

"How could you see it coming? A confidence fraud is just that... it builds confidence, so you do not to see it coming. I don't blame *you* for what Hobbs did. But what you continue to allow... this is your responsibility Irvin."

"I must be completely blind. I didn't see it... and I can't see this either. What you say: it is impossible..."

"I don't think so. I think we can find a way."

He repeated himself. "I just can't see it..."

"Then let me help. Let me help you see what I see! You don't have to do this alone."

"Joanna... after all this? How could you ever trust me? I wouldn't trust me! Why should you?"

"Let me help," she repeated and leant over and kissed him. "I love you Irvin Guthrie. Let me show you what I see. I remember someone saying once when I was stuck in mud and I couldn't move... that person told me that I didn't mean for it to happen but when it did, I did what I could to see it sorted. You have done that. That person also said, that 'two beasts are better than one'. Both of us should be able to sort our way through this. You are one very tough beast."

"Humph. You would use my own words against me."

"Not against you... *for* you. It wasn't just the heifer you saved that night in the bog. The way you didn't judge me for that mistake... that was life to me. Now it is my turn to help us get unstuck. This is not impossible just because it is not ideal or easy or quick. We didn't choose it, but now it is the case we need to do what it can together to find a way through it. We need to start."

"You're not making sense..."

"Hobbs expected us to run. I've heard the women talk. They are surprised we are still here. Others have come and left just as quick because of the way he screws down tight on outsiders. We are not the first. There is never any hard evidence of what goes down... just a lot of talk and angry newcomers who never stay. But he has bitten off more than he can chew when he took you on. We have not left... and we won't. We will stay and we will be a thorn in his side that will irritate just by being here to remind him of his fallibility."

"Fallibility? The man doesn't have one. He doesn't get anything other than his own way."

"Exactly: *that* is his Achilles' heel. His weakness is that he thinks he is invincible: cleverer than everyone else. But clever is not the only way to win a war. There is tenacity. Some of the ancient wars were won by sieges that took years. If we stay and build a life here for our family... in spite of all of this... he does not win. He intended to scam us and expected we would have a royal spit and then leave. If we just walk away like whimpering dogs, beaten with our tails between our legs, it reinforces his power to call all the shots. If we don't stay, he never has to look at what he has done. Instead, he gave us a footprint in this place. We have a right to be here now. We own this land. We are now 'local' whether he intended that or not. Actually, that was not so clever: *that* was his mistake."

"A siege: winning by not giving up..."

"You Mr Guthrie are very tenacious. You built Adele a house when you were married. I want you to build me a house... a strong house in this wide-open sunny place, so that we can make Bonnie and our baby a home."

"A house? With what? My bare hands and pixie dust? This is beyond even the wee Faeries. We have nothing. There is not a useful tree on this wasteland. We don't have the money to buy that sort of timber."

"But we have stone. Lots of stone. That is our resource. Build me a stone house."

He scoffed and when she said nothing, he turned to her amazed. "You are completely serious."

"Completely. Two stubborn mules are better than one." She leant over and kissed him again.

He turned his face away. "Stone?" He tried it on for size. "Using the very thing that makes this outlier unusable?"

"This is not a new idea: in the old country, castles down to shepherd huts are made out of stone. I know it can be done."

"But people don't build out of stone here."

"People use what they have. Most people have trees. We don't. But we have stone and a whole lot of time.

"Would you be happy with that? It sounds rough."

"You are losing perspective Irvin Guthrie. I am living in a donga with three walls and a canvas door. That's rough. This idea takes back what was taken: our capacity to control something. We just need to start."

He reached out his arm and placed it around her shoulders and leant back until they were lying down looking up at the clouds tinged in gold from the evening light. He said nothing for a long time. "You and your fancy ways are rubbing off on me. You have had to do a whole lot of rough Joanna, and I'm sorry about that. But if you can manage a rough old Guthrie... then perhaps a rough stone hut is not beyond you either. I'll do it. I'll build you a home out of this useless rock and make it something worth holding on to. It is just possible this baby of ours will have a stone castle to grow up in."

15.

Joanna's body was heavy with their child and she sat hard on the chair that had once stood under the window with a cushion for Adele. She spoke to Bonnie outside the lean-to, while she gathered the energy to prepare dinner. "Bonnie, go get your reader now while I prepare dinner. School night," said Joanna.

Irvin sat at a trestle bench looking at his house plans that were pinned down by a number of rocks. He looked at Joanna's drawn face and felt a twinge of remembrance at that familiar look of exhaustion he had seen in Adele many times during her illness. "Bon-Lass, you can leave the books for now. You and me: on dinner duty. We are giving Joanna the night off."

"But..."

"One night will not see you behind in your schooling." Irvin hunkered down in front of the fire-pit. "Besides, this may well be the last time we cook dinner on this outside hearth, and we need to make a smile-moment out of it. The cookhouse is all but done. Tomorrow we break her in..."

She eased her weight gratefully in the chair while they stoked the fire and started to gather things from the meat safe. "Our new cookhouse seems like a fine thoroughbred horse compared to this old donkey of a thing. It is a very flash cookhouse," she observed.

"Fancy enough for your fancy ways then?" he said good-naturedly.

"I'm thinking a fancy cookhouse will still only produce the kind of plain fare that you're used to. I am not a fancy cook."

He grinned. "We are plain folk here..."

The smoke rising from the fire had a satisfying feel of family. She sat for a while and then restlessly stood up and went inside the humpy and collected the washing basket and took the clothes off the string line that was strung between the humpy and a spindly low tree. She sat and folded the clothes, and then put them away in the makeshift cupboards made of boxes. She tidied around the bunks and swept the hard, compact floor, rearranged the chairs and trestle to the side of the fire pit. She raked away leaves and the occasional bone that Tuck had imported to gnaw on. She sat down again... and then found herself sorting dirty laundry that needed to be done on the morrow. She shifted again to relieve the pressure on her back, and then restlessly went inside and selected two books put aside for Bonnie's reading list. She grabbed the water pail, went down to the well, drew some water and took it back to the camp. She set it down and helped Bonnie finish setting the table for their meal.

Irvin stirred the stew. "It won't be long before we're ready to start the big house," he said.

Bonnie cheered. "Just like the third little pig. We will all be safe in our little stone house. Though we will be four little pigs soon."

Irvin shook his head and grinned. "Everything is a story book..."

"It will be a stone house where the big bad wolf doesn't get stuck in the chimney... or fuzzy little possums either," Bonnie laughed.

He chuckled with her. "We have come quite a way since that first day Miss Joanna arrived. And you are right. This little pig is going to build you a house that will not be blown over... and will keep the wildlife out. Clever little pig..." He lifted the pot out of the coals to begin serving. He paused, suspended over the fire. "Pigs? How about that..." he quietly mused to himself. The corner of his shirt dangled in the coals and flared into flame. He dropped the pot and Joanna jumped up and grabbed the pail and doused him in water. He pulled off his shirt, beat out the flames; his forearm, red and scalded. Joanna quickly went to find some salve, and then stopped for a moment to catch her breath. She applied a bandage made from strips of old washed linen while Irvin tried to distract Bonnie by asking her to salvage their dinner amongst ash and water. There was little left in the pot except gravy... so she cut some bread they could use to mop it up. Basic dinner tonight.

Joanna rubbed her back and noticed how Irvin had handled this challenge so calmly. No throwing buckets or swearing or kicking Tuck in frustration. This was the family that she had met, where possums were dislodged, and work was part of the pulling together in the face of all sorts of challenges. Fighting the elements together. Building together. She would never underestimate the privilege of this kind of family.

Irvin said grace, and they tucked into the leftovers as if it was a three-course spread. "So, Bon-Lass, you managed to retrieve dinner for us. When we are using the cookhouse, hopefully these little pigs will not have to resort to bread and gravy for dinner just because I knocked the pot."

"Hmm. Learning takes practice. Practice makes perfect. Since the cookhouse was practice; this house will be perfect."

Joanna smiled; her tutoring mantras had become part of their family language. She winced once or twice during dinner, eating her bread slowly. Perhaps lifting the water bucket from the well and then tossing it all over her husband had other implications this evening and she paused to rub her back firmly. The well was the first project Irvin finished. It had been metaphoric almost... digging to find water, under all the dirt and rock and pain and anger.

That well-water, and process to access it, had been healing. It offered life. In just a few months all their stalled momentum had started rolling and now was moving along at a steady rate.

Bonnie finished her dinner and retired to her bunk with her reader and a lamp. Joanna collected the plates in a bucket and then put it down. She was aware that her cramps had become contractions, and now at regular intervals her abdomen was rock hard. She sat again and coughed a little. "Irvin?"

His head was filled with plans of stone and mortar. "Hmm? What if I rotated the aspect to face north? It would be not directly facing west in summer. The sun comes up over there now. Don't want so much sun we fry like lard in a pan."

She smiled at that. In just a short while, the details were coming together. "Irvin..."

"Yes. That would be better." He sat down with another slab of bread and threw the crusts to Tuck.

"Irvin... I think this baby..." She paused and looked away holding her breath.

He didn't look up but stared at the plans with a frown. He paused and nodded, tracing some of the detail with his finger. "This baby is exactly what we need just now."

She restlessly got up and walked around. "Oh indeed? I remember you saying this baby was a problem that you did not care for." Irvin looked up into her eyes. She acknowledged this was his apology and nodded. She came over and kissed his brow. "Thank you, Mr Guthrie," she whispered.

"What for? This hasn't been easy."

"I wasn't looking for easy. I was looking for you."

"Well, you've had me for worse. I am working on better." He reached out and gently placed his hand protectively on her abdomen. "For all of us..."

"Hmmm. I think we will have to work on that tonight." She gasped and gripped his shoulder as she breathed through a contraction. "This baby is coming tonight... and from all the reports I have been given from the mothers at the school, it's not going to be easy."

જ્ઞBDCଓન

16.

Hobbs walked down the street with Jimbo in his shadow. They went into the pub and sat at their designated table. It gave them the view of the bar and the other tables, and the comings and goings of the townspeople through the window. They caught the end of a conversation that continued at the bar, unaware of the scrutiny. "... what he's doing on that pile of gravel is nothing short of an act of the Almighty: making something out of nothing."

His mate philosophically stared into his tankard. "I would never have laid a bet on him beating a plough shear out of that joint. He's running pigs on the flat... charging Joe the butcher to dispose of his offal... and then feeding it to 'em. Then he sells them back to Joe for butchering. I reckon the man's got nerve."

The last of the trio stared at his cheap beer, cloudy and headless. "It's the pigs that done it. Had an uncle that done the same thing on a slab of dirt that was like the cold-stone-marble you lie cadavers on. In no time he was growing corn in that paddock so tall he lost his draught-horse in it. Guthrie's savvy. Heard he's reckoning on growing a market garden with pumpkins you can live in."

That observation deserved a chuckle. He swigged his beer and offered another tuppence worth of wisdom. "Pumpkins might be better than rocks. Softer."

"Got rocks in his head, in my mind. Took him a month of Sundays just to build an outhouse."

"Well... he sat on that plot for nearly a year, sulking around like a toddler with a fully-loaded nappy. I would have bet my last bob that he'd rot there or split through. But since that little tyke of his come along... he reckons he's got plans. Not my idea of a good time... but I give him points for hanging-on-in. I heard his missus..."

The barman pushed him another drink and subtly glanced over at Hobbs staring them down. Jimbo was flexing his fist. Without missing a beat, he took the drink and glanced in the reflection of the glass behind the bar. "Damn out-a'-towners," he said a little louder, as he downed his drink and concluded with emphasis, "Will never be part of this place that's for sure." He thumped his tankard on the bar and bolted. His mates followed not far behind. And the barman breathed a little easier as he wiped the bench and watched out of the corner of his eye, as the tension in Jimbo's fist stretched and relaxed.

≈≈∞)(∞≈≈

Soon. It is hard to be patient when 'soon' is the ever-elusive invitation. Joanna and Bonnie walked over to where the plan of the house was pegged out and foundation footings were being sunk. Irvin was heaping stacks of stone at strategic points around the site. Joanna put little Harry down from her hip and he toddled around the piles of rock positioned there for his climbing entertainment, and Bonnie trailed after him.

"Irvin? I want to talk to you about something."

"Fire away," he said without looking up.

"I saw Mrs Hollander in town today. She said that the school term starts soon, and they still do not have a teacher since Mr Renmark left at the end of last year. She wanted me to consider filling in while they wait for the other applicant to arrive. She said she would speak to the committee."

He stopped emptying the barrow and wiped his hands down his trousers. "You can't."

"Why not? I think I can."

"You have Harry. And you're still feeding him."

"I'm thinking of weaning him. It's time."

"You still can't. Shouldn't. It isn't done."

"I work here. How is it different? Except there they will pay me."

"Well, it isn't right. You're married. It's my job to provide."

"This is about helping the children, not whether you are good at providing."

"Are you never satisfied Joanna? What have I got to do?" His voice held a harsh frustrated edge.

"Irvin, I am grateful! I could never have considered this before... but I feel now we are on track again: you and me, it could be a possibility. And this just came up. I didn't go looking for it."

"You teach Bonnie. That should be enough."

"It is because of Bonnie that they suggested it. They see what she can do. For someone so young she is tutoring the others. She shouldn't have to do that when she is meant to be the student. Besides, they will pay me... and it could be a little extra for the house. I'm sure it won't be for long."

"Bah. It's nonsense. What are you going to do with Harry?"

"I'll take him with me. The committee may not even approve it. Like you said: I'm a woman: married with a child. It is the general opinion that our shrivelled brains, shrivel a little more when we marry... and a little more when we give birth."

He looked at her then and shook his head. "You may just be proof their notion is true. Why would you even be bothered with that lot?"

"You know I've always wanted to teach. That hasn't changed just because Reverend Brasheur decided I needed to be a man to have such an ambition, or because I put a band of jewellery on my fourth finger."

"Won't matter anyway. They will never go for it."

"Mrs Hollander has very convincing ways."

"Hollander works for Hobbs."

"Her husband does. And this whole community is connected to Gumleigh Station in some way. That is a reality of living here Irvin. Even us." When she said it, she immediately wished she could retract it. And she quickly poured herself tea from the billy and said a prayer under her breath as she set out their lunch from the basket she had brought over from the cookhouse. "It would only be for a short time anyway."

He sat for a while staring into his mug. "There is a kind of sweet irony in you teaching their kids. Even I can appreciate that," he admitted. "Well. Sure. Throw your hat in the ring. But don't be mad when they turn you down... or turn you out... or rip you off... or rob you blind. The next guy will be along soon enough, even one who hasn't cut his twelve-year-old molars yet."

Joanna nodded and turned away and breathed a sigh of relief. When the door at Reverend Brasheur's school was slammed, she never imagined it being prised open ever again. But there was just a little gap visible here and the light was showing through. Was it possible that after all this time, her very old and dormant dream was being dusted off? Had her dream had been preserved for this season? Was it possible when so many things were against it? Women don't teach, when there are men who can do it. Women give up their jobs, when they marry. Women don't pursue employment when they have a family. That was the trifecta that meant her teaching dream had been buried. But now... now it was rising out of the barren ground like the beautiful plans for a stone house.

∾• இ ✽ ✽ ❀ ✽ ✽ இ •∾

17.

Joanna acknowledged that, for some reason, much of her life rotated around the idea of filling in. The fill-in carer and fill-in nurse. The fill-in tutor and fill-in governess. The fill-in wife. The fill-in mother. The fill-in teacher. But each of those fill-in moments had brought richness to her life. She walked up the hill with Bonnie beside her carrying a little swag of books. The school year had started smoothly, and the lack of an official appointment was hardly noticed. Part of the arrangement was that little Harry would have someone look after him while Joanna took her classes. One of the young mothers was given that responsibility and they were on their way to collect him after class. Bonnie chatted amiably about their day and the prospect of their new teacher, which had been the constant topic of speculation since they had heard a family moved into that nice house across from the General Store. They had waited all week for the kids to appear at school, and their absence became a major discussion topic with many questions.

Gumleigh felt obligated to stamp all newcomers 'approved' before they could attain the status of being locals. This social filter meant that newcomers rarely achieved that endorsed status unless they were moving to Gumleigh as direct employees of Hobbs. It was a process that the Guthrie family had defied, but now they were edging their way into the community anyway.   A conversation here; lending a hand there. Mostly they kept to themselves. Joanna's offer to fill-in at the school so the school term could start without interruption was considered an agreeable endeavour; at least by those mothers who valued the idea of their children improving. Although, for the most part, the Guthries were still considered outsiders. They didn't fit the Gumleigh normal.

Joanna was confident that Mrs Hollander would clarify the new family's unknown position as soon as she knew the situation. She had appointed herself as the community's Town-Cryer... the voice that shared information in lieu of a local gazette. The new schoolteacher would qualify as one of the acceptable ones, and the Gurthrie's status as outsiders would resume. However, the silence around this family's arrival was certainly something of an oddity. They were not trumpeting their connection, their status, or their employment.

Joanna and Bonnie, with little Harry in toe, turned onto the track that ran out to their block when they came across an unfamiliar man walking along with his wife, and two children who were not too far from Bonnie's age.

"Good afternoon," smiled Joanna. "We are just walking home from school."

The woman responded warmly to her greeting. "I'm Mrs Orford. My husband, Mr Hallum Orford. We have moved into the house opposite the general store."

"Then you must be the new schoolteacher we have heard so much about? Welcome to Gumleigh Mr and Mrs Orford."

The children sniggered. The woman placed a hand on their shoulders requiring restraint in their manners. "This is my son Jeremy, and my daughter Louisa. No, my husband is not the teacher."

"You have no appointment? Then why are you here?" asked Joanna with unrestrained curiosity. Bonnie dumped her schoolbooks and lured the children away to play tag.

Mr Orford smiled at the children. "Well, we desired a change of pace and weather. This seemed a likely place."

"Well, I never! We came to Gumleigh for exactly the same circumstance. I trust your time in Gumleigh offers you everything you are looking for."

Mrs Orford seemed to have found her tongue. "I take it that they have not yet made a permanent appointment at the school if you are asking if the job is my Hallum's? I heard they had a temporary teacher. We thought we would wait until the permanent teacher was placed before we enrolled Jerry and Louisa. That would be less disrupting on their schooling."

Hmm. Joanna was not sure whether she should be slighted by their reservations. The rumours that these were people of position seemed legitimate. They were dressed well. They were sure of their own opinions. But Joanna saw something else... now they were displaced and marooned on a rural island call Gumleigh. Then she smiled. She could relate to that as well. More common ground. "Actually, I am the substitute teacher."

"Oh! Quite shocking! No disrespect intended of course, I just meant, well... since you are a woman. It is unexpected that's all," she quickly qualified.

Joanna raised her brow and somehow didn't feel she needed to be offended by her frankness. "Yes, so it seems. And to top it off... the controversy gets bigger: I am a wife and a mother! That is Bonnie, and this is little Harry."

"Oh! Well, I never. I didn't actually think that Gumleigh was at all a progressive place. It seems so very conservative. If I could tell my suffragette ladies this, they would be very impressed by your endeavours, Mrs Guthrie."

"It is probably less impressive than I wish. Gumleigh is very conservative; but it is also very desperate. It is hard to get professional people to relocate to these smaller communities. Somehow what is unthinkable in other places just becomes normal here because of necessity. I did not want the education of my daughter Bonnie... and the other children, to be compromised by the lack of a suitable tutor.

As soon as the position can be filled, of course, I will be stepping down. The last successful candidate withdrew, so my services were extended. I just supposed that you were that next teacher Mr Orford. You dress like a professional man. My apologies for my assumptions."

He shrugged and looked over to where the children had abandoned tag and were now using sticks they found by the track to play hockey with a stone. "Well, we are not here to displace you. Be reassured I have no appointment at the school."

"Is this something that you would consider? Are you qualified to teach?"

"I am qualified, but not as a teacher." They talked while they walked the road, and Joanna felt this family was more like neighbours than anyone else she had met in this town.

"Well, since we have spoken with you, perhaps the children might enrol," offered Mrs Orford tentatively.

Joanna was increasingly delighted with this family. She gave the details on when to come to the school. It felt like she was throwing crumbs to migratory ducks swimming on the river. Perhaps if she threw enough crumbs they would stay and not move on.

They met on the road most days. The children were enrolled, and Joanna offered to walk with them after school to meet up with their parents so they could maintain their routine of an afternoon stroll.   They would chat about school and the kids took the time to play an extra game. One particularly warm day, Joanna offered a cool drink of well-water and some shade. "Please. Come and meet my husband. You are not far from our block. He is in the depths of a building project at the moment."

Mr Orford looked up quickly, and his eyes lit with interest. "He is a builder?"

"Well, he is building so... yes... I guess so. He built his previous home, but this project has different challenges. He is building our house... out of stone."

"Stone hey? I would love to meet him," and Mr Orford strode ahead and whistled to the children.

Joanna smiled as she walked with Mrs Orford behind. It was refreshing to find company oblivious to the Gumleigh prejudice against "out-of-towners". Perhaps it was because their presence was unaccounted for and that put them in an uncertain social category. Irvin shook hands and walked Orford around his worksite. He showed him over the cookhouse and soon they were delving into more and more technical issues of working with stone. Irvin had many questions and it seemed Hal Orford had answers. In a short time, they had covered a full spectrum of subjects, and Orford even offered Irvin his favourite mortar recipe, the parts of lime needed to stabilise a workable compound.

"I've seen places just crumble because the mud they used was virtually just that... mud. No strength."

Irvin shaded his eyes from the afternoon sun. "Well, you do know building it seems..."

"Been doing it for a while. Actually, that's why we are here. I'm to oversee a local project."

"Are you now?" said Irvin with a good-natured smile.

"Don't expect we'll be staying on after it's done."

"Won't you now?" said Irvin.

"On to where the next project takes me. This one won't be stone. Man, I really like what you've done here! I could see some of these features being used in my project."

"My wife seems to think that you'd make a good schoolteacher."

"Don't know why they would be trying to replace her. She seems to be doing a good job. My wife is cautious... but I can't see the harm. It's just reading and numbers. It is not like they are learning anything technical at their age."

"Is it now?" Irvin turned and took a drink from his canvas water bag. Was the man impervious to the fact he was talking to this particular teacher's husband? Even if Irvin had been reluctant about Joanna taking the job, he defended Joanna's commitment to the role. "Well, I'm guessing even the best of engineers start by counting to ten."

"Ha, that is true."

The following week Orford checked in as he promised and handed over his preferred mortar recipe. "Use this and I could guarantee this little place will outlast the Roman Colosseum. It's the best I've come across."

Irvin shook his hand gratefully. Orford's coming seemed providential because he had many more questions. And they dived into talking shop.

As he was leaving, Orford paused. "I'm assembling a building crew for that project I was telling you about. Are you wanting to contract some labour? I could do with a man like yourself."

"Nah. Got my hands full here. Never been one to work for another. Prefer my own company."

"Shame. I've costed Hobbs' project, so I have the option to be generous."

Irvin turned back and stared at him. "You are working for Hobbs?" But of course. Hobbs owns everyone. It explained why Orford had been tight lipped about what he was doing here. Irvin considered him suspiciously. Was he some sort of Hobbs' spy? But their conversations around building with stone had seemed genuine, and Hal had been open and generous with input into this building project. He never had any sense he was being set up or sabotaged. But then – that had happened before.

Hal made a point of emphasising that he had contracted the Hobbs' job on his own terms. It made Irvin pause. He conceded there was something in Orford's independent status that meant he held himself apart from the local parochialism. And Irvin knew himself well enough to know that if he had known of his connection with Hobbs from the start, he would have shut him out. Was it possible not to condemn everyone who touched the tainted Hobbs' barrel? Irvin spat on the ground and made no attempt to hide his scorn. "Bah. The man's a snake. Be careful you don't end up staked out to feed his vultures."

"I've asked around. He provided solid references."

"Then you haven't been listening. He is silver tongued, and as smooth as port wine. A reference you pay for means nothing in the end."

Orford eyed him carefully. Hal didn't doubt Guthrie's assessment was personal, even if it was not objective. There are usually good reasons for that.

Irvin shrugged. Well at least he offered Orford the courtesy of a warning. That was something no one bothered to give him. But he still had to be true to what he knew, and he knew Hobbs could not be trusted. "Well good luck to you then. Watch your back though."

≈☙◖◗☙≈

18.

The community was buzzing. Mrs Hollander had published her version of events. Orford was a very accomplished engineer and architect right here in Gumleigh, and Mr Hobbs had contracted him to oversee the building of a new Overseer's residence. That was quite the feather in Jimbo's hat. He strutted the streets and became a little bit louder and a big bit more obnoxious, if that was even possible. Mr Hobbs regarded him so well that he had rewarded him with a *new* house! That was an idea that sat well with his heavy fists and dull intellect.

Irvin just shook his head. It made no sense to him that an overseer would ever need anything other than the residence that already stood on that block. He scorned their basic dismissal of perfection while he picked another barrow-load of rocks and distributed them around his site.

Orford tried a couple of times to engage Irvin with offers of hire. Irvin never relented. Although the offers started to escalate, it was easy enough to ignore them when he knew the contract was connected with Hobbs. Even easier when it was Jimbo's place that was getting all the attention. However, Orford's genuine interest in construction meant he continued to pop in on Irvin to admire his progress. He gave him unsolicited engineering advice which Irvin was sensible enough to take on board.

Building Jimbo's new place was like a traditional barn-raising of the plain-folk. It was a small house on a small block, that quickly took shape. In Irvin's assessment, nothing about it was better. Yet Jimbo and his wife were jubilant. It was new! And while the new cottage emerged before the town's eyes like a miraculous sandcastle on a barmy afternoon at the beach, Irvin plugged away and placed stone on stone. Joanna was there to encourage and support, in between giving lessons at the school. Something within her celebrated that her teaching dream had become reality in ways that were more enriching than the cold little parish school supervised by the Brasheurs. Life for the Guthries now held a pleasant sort of rhythm.

Orford came one day and sat with Irvin perched on a part wall that was slowly rising out of the foundations while they had a drink together. "I've got the next phase of this project coming up. Got some stuff I need to get rid of. I notice you dispose of the butcher's waste... and you have a wagon. What if I pay you to get rid of some of this rubble?"

Irvin smirked. This was a man who did not give up easily. But he wasn't one to give in either. Not now. "So where do you think I would dump rubbish? I don't have access to anywhere that needs fill. And I'm not using this place as a tip. I'm trying to clean it up."

Orford looked subdued and grinned a little. "Well... what if it was less like junk and more akin to... building timbers and the kind. What you do with it after I pay you to get rid of it, is entirely none of my business." Orford mapped out the job.

Irvin shook his head in a kind of stupor. "He is pulling it down?"

"I have to clear the whole site."

"So that's why Jimbo got the new hut. Hobbs is using the site to build himself a palace."

"He wants Gumleigh to have a Homestead in keeping with his grandiose ideas of a land baron. That block has the best outlook. And you're right, it's going to be flash... really flash." He looked out over Guthrie's lot, and saw more potential through the eyes of an engineer and architect. "So, my question remains... can I contract you to dispose of the 'rubble'. If you oversee the demolition, we can make sure the timbers are taken off cleanly and don't end up so splintered they'd be good for nothing but fuel for your cookhouse."

They shook hands on it. Irvin grinned. "Orford, you are something else. You've been working on getting me to sign on for you ever since you arrived."

Orford shrugged. "You don't work for me, or Hobbs. You're like me: an independent contractor. Perchance this might be part way... towards righting a wrong. Not that I would dare poke my nose in that particular rat-trap."

Irvin looked at him. "You're different to their lot. Why are you doing this?"

"Your wife was the first person to speak nicely to my Lydia. Your Bonnie was the first kid to play with my Jerry and Louisa. To start with, the townsfolk kept their distance because they were not sure we were Hobbs endorsed. But since people have found out we are only passing through, no one is really interested in getting to know us. So, it is not money or reputation that has made us feel at home here. It is good people with big hearts. You have every reason to be snarky about me contracting for Hobbs, but you haven't dumped me in with his kind, even though we are only going to be here for a just short time. That's more the measure of a man than whose payroll he's on. Besides. I like buildings. This here, this is something special."

Irvin tipped out the dregs of his tea. "We ain't fancy people here."

Orford grinned. "Simple folk with a decent sized wagon. Sounds like a we have a deal."

⁂

<h1 style="text-align:center">19.</h1>

"So, I got to thinking about what could be done with extra timber. I played around a bit and drafted up some ideas using your stone walls as the feature of the house," said Orford, restlessly holding a role of plans.

"You re-planned my house?"

"Brainstorming mainly; on paper. No obligation for you to look at them of course."

"Did you now? You are tarred with the same brush as Joanna. She was doing the same thing for months when we first came here. Every time I turned around there was a different drawing of some sort of stone house. Said she was drawing what she could see."

"And what you could not," said Joanna with a smile. "Irvin is what I call 'an executioner'... he can execute anything I throw at him. Dreaming is easy for me. Would you mind if I had a look?"

Orford looked at Irvin who shrugged and went back to his rocks. Hal unrolled the paper and laid it out on the top of a barrel. "Oh, my goodness!" exclaimed Joanna. "I thought I could dream. But *this* is a dream! And you say the demolition will provide all the timber needed to make this? That is completely extraordinary!"

Irvin sighed. He put down the rock in his hand and came to look over her shoulder. He knew he was being lured into their little schemes. Joanna smiled and kissed Irvin goodbye. She bundled Bonnie and Harry together and headed out for school.

Irvin looked over the plan and raised his brow. "So, what is that going to cost me... using a plan like this?"

"What do you mean?"

"Well, you are some highfalutin architect from the Big Smoke who has got Hobbs paying through his gold-plated teeth for your services. A plan like this doesn't come cheap."

"Hmm. What you say is true. I have consulted on many high-profile projects. But a man needs to have some fun. I don't charge for fun."

"Fun?"

"Yeah. What you are doing here: with local stone, using what you have to improve your lot... this is magic. It's inspired me to play around with it some, just to see what could be added in. Even if it is resourceful, doesn't mean it has to be shabby. What I see here... even though it is not big... this is definitely not shabby.

"You know Orford... you don't have a way with words."

"True. But I know buildings. I want to give you this. These stone-walls will last forever. Solid as the Great Wall of China. The rest is... well, that is just dressing it up for the Missus."

"This is pretty flash, for people who ain't fancy. It makes Jimbo's new place look like a chook-coop."

"Jimbo's place was throwing him a bone so Hobbs could level the hill-site without a fight. But Hobbs doesn't need to know that he's not the only one who will get the best consulting in this town. This plan here... it's not large, but I worked out what could be done with the type and amount of timber you get from the site. Never had to work back to front like that before. But I wanted to be sure you have everything you need to do this. It is just what Joanna said... executing what's on the paper."

"Joanna said something to me once: that there is more than one way to secure the treasure than storming the gates. I like that idea – this is a treasure map. This is the backdoor into the castle. It's a good plan. You sign me a statement to say I've got all the rights to use this... and I'm in."

"I meant what I said. It's yours."

"Then sign it over. I trusted someone once... and even with all the paperwork it fell over. That's made me nervous. Nothing personal."

"Done. I'll do it now." He pulled a pen and pot from his satchel and scrawled his signature over the top of the plan. "All rights and property of... dated and signed. "Good enough?"

Irvin nodded. "That'll do it..." and without hardly a pause they went to work, and began to pace out the site, where to put the additional footings and what the next stages were in executing the plan.

It was late in the afternoon when Orford left. Guthrie sat on a partially built stone wall with Tuck lying in the shade beside him. He adjusted his hat and took a drink from his canvas water bag, surveying his block. "Wide open spaces," he mused. The cramped little stone box he was going to build didn't fit Joanna's preference for open, sunny, spacious, but she had never offered anything other than enthusiastic encouragement. However, this plan... this plan had everything! This would be her fancy castle... a home for their family. And yes, he understood now... the treasure was his family.

He looked out over the paddock where his mules were hugging low stunted trees for shade. Closer, there were Bonnie's chooks scratching in the dirt, and the pigs freeranging the paddock near the gully, with Ticka, the heifer, who was now in calf. He could see rows of seedlings sprouting green lines in the start of his market garden along the creek. Just now it looked more like a back yard vege-patch, but it was a beginning. Some divine hand had reached down to pull him out of the bog, and he had been rescued. His feet had been set on a firm rock. This rocky knoll was the solid, spacious place he had prayed for. He shook his head at that. What he thought was a curse, had turned into something good. Really good. Tuck's ears pricked and he abruptly ran out towards the road. Guthrie stood up; his eyes followed the dog as it raced out to meet his family returning from school. This was the highlight of his day, seeing Joanna walking up the track with Harry on her hip, his tired little legs not able to make the last of the walk home. His challenge was to take Orford's plan and make it a reality. And watching Bonnie race ahead to meet Tuck, laughing as she threw him a stick... that was his smile.

Joanna reached Irvin, and with relief handed Harry over. He bounced Harry onto his shoulders, and they walked over to the donga and sat together in the shade with a drink. She spoke about her day and her students, and how some of the mothers just couldn't understand why homework should be a priority when there were chores to be done. Joanna paused as she became aware of his silence. She looked at him quickly, checking her words. Was he retreating again? But what she saw was not a stony, sullen withdrawal, but a smile of affection in his eyes. "What is it Mr Guthrie?"

Harry squirmed from his arms and toddled over to where Bonnie was playing with Tuck. "It is you..."

"Me...?"

He reached out and traced her skin with his rough hand, lingering over the wedding band on her finger. "I came home one day to my tired little cabin. My wife is sick. My daughter is growing up too quickly, without being able to read a word. My life was closing in and I had no idea what to do. I never told you of the prayer I prayed in the paddock that day. I was asking... demanding perhaps... that God would give us space... space just to be a family... like we dreamed of in the beginning. And there you were, standing in the middle of the track, looking like the Reverend had sent you to Africa. And although it is not what you wanted; you made that happen. I had no idea that the time I had left with Adele was so short, but you created space for us, Joanna. Bonnie... the same. When I thought my world had collapsed, there you were again. Just now, listening to you talk about the kids at the school, you are doing it there too. Everywhere you go... you open things up and create space for them to flourish. I am very grateful, Joanna, very grateful that God sent you and answered my prayer."

"Oh Irvin... thank you." She took another drink and swallowed. "I have only thought of my life as gap-filler. The fill-in. The make-do. What you have said... that..." There was a catch in her voice and emotion filled her eyes. "Thank you! You have done the same for me. You open up my life to all sorts of possibilities."

Irvin pulled her in closer. "Do you know, Joanna, really know, that you are not fill-in for me? You are not make-do. You are my treasure..."

She sighed contentedly as he gently tilted her chin and kissed her. They sat together and looked out over the emerging walls of their home rising out of the barren ground. The future looked wide open... a spacious place. Their lot was indeed blessed.

The end

❦␍❧

Next up in the Guthrie's Lot Series

Guthrie's Lot #2: A Level Path

She looked down the laneway and realised she needed to know which path to take. Perhaps that was what she needed, even more than a holiday. Space to clear the fog and find direction.

Iris Guthrie isn't running away – not really. It's the hip 1960s, and she has dreams of adventure and excitement and a journey to England is just what she needs to clear her head and help her find her path.

David is not the adventurous type, so following Iris to England is not something either of them expected.

Will Iris see through the witty and charming, but ultimately selfish, Stan, or will Dave travel back to Australia alone as Iris finds her way to *A Level Path?*